THE EARL'S BITTER SECRET

CHARLOTTE DARCY

FAIR HAVENS BOOKS

COPYRIGHT

INTRODUCTION

This is my third longer Regency Romance and I hope you enjoy it. Each book has changed, following the wonderful comments and feedback I have gained from you my amazing readers. You have helped give me the confidence to share my stories and have helped me improve my writing along the way. I feel truly blessed to have you along on this adventure with me and thank you all from the bottom of my heart.

This book can be read alone but if you wish to read them in order the two previous books in this series are also available:

The Broken Duke – Mended by Love & The BlueStocking, the Earl, & the Author

I hope you enjoy this book and as a thank you for being such wonderful readers I would like to offer you a FREE short, clean Regency romance. You can get it by joining my exclusive newsletter **here.**

God Bless,

Charlotte Darcy

CHAPTER 1

"*B*ut the Earl of Pennington, are you quite sure, Mary?" William Porter wore the expression of a man who already knew the argument was lost. Still, he was Mary's father, and it was essential that he be sure she was doing the right thing.

"The Earl of Pennington will be as good an employer as any, Papa," Mary replied, before reaching out to touch her father's kindly face.

"But my dear girl, you have no need to work now, nor shall you ever have. I'm afraid that is the part which I find the hardest to comprehend, my dear." William Porter shrugged a little and smiled disarmingly at his daughter. He knew well how strident she could be and hoped to avoid a telling off at all costs.

"You're right, Father, in that I do not need to work for financial reasons. However, I still very much have a *need* to work. Ever since the Dame school closed, I have felt somewhat bereft, and no amount of money shall cure that feeling."

Much had changed in the two years since William Porter had found himself the somewhat startled heir to the vast Stonewell Shipping company fortune. In many ways, life had improved considerably. Whilst the Porter family had certainly not been poor by any stretch of the imagination, they most certainly had not been what could be considered wealthy. Their sudden change in fortunes had meant that William Porter had been able to quit his work as an accountant and live a much more restful and pleasant life filled with new hope and new hobbies.

Whilst Mary had very much rejoiced in their new-found wealth, she had found she suffered greatly when the tiny Dame school she had run from their home had come to an end. In truth, she had only ever had nine pupils, some of whom rather came and went, and two of whom were her own sisters, but the teaching of those children had given Mary such a great sense of purpose. When her father had employed a governess for Eliza and Peggy, and the last of her remaining pupils had drifted away, either into work or new towns, Mary's life seemed to have ground to a halt.

"Oh, my dear girl, perhaps I should never have employed a governess for Eliza and Peggy." William Porter's look of concern turned to one of barely concealed guilt.

"Oh, Father! Please do not decide upon blaming yourself in any way. And in truth, Eliza and Peggy are now fourteen and twelve-years-old, and would not have been needing me for very much longer anyway. I daresay it is time to spread my wings a little and broaden my horizons."

"Well, what about travel? That would broaden your horizons, and it would be a wonderful adventure."

"How wonderfully kind you are, Papa, to think of such fulfilling pastimes for me. But I am afraid that the teaching of children is not something I necessarily see as work. Rather it is something of a vocation for me, and in that much, it rather has merit all of its own. Obviously, the money shall be as nothing to me now, for since you sold the shipping company I have more money than I could ever dream of spending."

"And what of marriage, Mary? I know you have always forsworn the idea, but now that you are twenty, perhaps it is time you thought about it?" Mary would have been annoyed at her father's comment had his face not been so comically nervous. Furthermore, it seemed to her that he had backed away a little, taking a few steps closer to the door.

"Papa! Am I really such a gorgon that you are ready to run?" Mary could not help but laugh.

"Well, sometimes, my darling child." Seeing that his daughter had not taken his proposal as a tremendous insult, William Porter slowly and steadily began to make his way back into the room.

"In truth, when I was younger, I really had no interest whatsoever in romance and marriage. I cannot blame you for your careful questioning." Mary chuckled a little. "And I must admit that, lately, I have rather thought about marriage, obviously to the right person. You see, I am determined to wait for the right person, Papa. You see, now that I have money, I have the greatest fear of a man marrying me for it. You know how I am, and you know very well that I should not be easy with the idea of a man marrying me and taking control of every part of my life, my wealth included."

"But not all men are like that, my dear."

"No, Papa, I know they are not... and yet you see, I really must be absolutely sure before marrying. The money that you gave me after you sold the shipping company has offered me such a wonderful opportunity for an independent life, and I shall never know quite how to thank you for that."

"There is no need. It would break my heart, Mary my dear, to think that the money which would offer you such independence might also render you entirely alone."

"Not alone, Papa, but rather with the determination to make the right choice."

"I just worry that your *right choice* might come far too late. Forgive me, my child, but I cannot bear to think of you alone."

"I am but twenty years, Papa, and anyone who thinks that a woman of twenty-three or twenty-four is too old to marry, then he was never the right man for me in the first place. Do you see?"

"Well, I think I'm beginning to, Mary." William smiled and nodded, although Mary was not entirely sure that her father understood her motives, either in work or matrimony.

"Anyway, now that you are married again, my dear Papa, it is most certainly time that your second eldest daughter leaves home," Mary said with a little laugh.

The sadness and melancholy which seemed to have clung to her father in the years since her mother had died in childbirth, had slowly but surely melted away. Mary gathered that it was a mixture of things; the passage of time, the peace of mind which came from sudden wealth, and seeing his eldest daughter, Katherine, happily married to the Duke of

Arleton. His relationship with a local widow, Ann Turner, had developed slowly over the last two years, culminating in their eventual marriage just two months before.

"Now you know that Ann would be overjoyed to keep you here forever, Mary!" William said, laughing heartily.

"Yes, Papa." Mary laughed too. "She is such a dear woman, and I cannot tell you how happy it makes me to see the two of you so content."

Mary was extremely fond of Ann, and the feeling was mutual. Ann had nursed her own husband through a dreadful illness and had been alone for many years. She knew very well of William's suffering, having dealt with very much the same thing herself. Never having had children of her own, Ann had thoroughly enjoyed playing mother to Eliza and Peggy and even, on occasion, Mary herself. In truth, Mary was not going to be leaving home lightly. However, as much as she felt something akin to a stone sitting in her stomach every time she thought of leaving her loving family behind, still Mary knew in her heart that she must follow her vocation and make a life for herself.

"Now, to get back to my original question, are you sure that the Earl of Pennington is an employer you should find yourself happy with?"

"It is not the Earl I need to be happy with, Papa, but merely the work. He has two young children of only four years of age, and the opportunity to start a child's education, rather than to come into it some way down the line, is very much a challenge that I welcome."

"But surely the humor of your employer, good or bad, must have some sort of effect on your life. After all, it is not simply a job from which you walk away as the sun sets, is it? You shall be living there, Mary, and I cannot see how your employer would not be the absolute deciding factor in amongst it all."

"I daresay that you are referring to his rather surly countenance, Papa?" Mary rose from the kitchen table and set a pan of water to boil on the stove. Despite the fact that the family had now employed a cook and maid to assist them in their daily lives, years of self-sufficiency were a hard habit to break. Mary often found herself making tea and tidying up as if they had never become wealthy. Sometimes it soothed her, and she so hated to be idle. William and Mary's habit of taking breakfast at the kitchen table and remaining there for some time afterward had also not been broken. Initially, the new staff had found it somewhat disconcerting behavior, but they very quickly got used to their new employers.

As Mary spooned tea leaves into the pot, she felt a little tug at her heart to think that not many more of her mornings would be spent thus. In the days when all adult members of the family had been working, mornings had been a time of high activity, hurried breakfasts, and a certain amount of camaraderie and togetherness. In the two years since the work had become unnecessary, the camaraderie and togetherness at breakfast time had remained, and Mary knew that she would miss that above all things when she finally came face-to-face with a new kind of life.

"If I am honest, Mary, then yes. I have heard that the Earl has always been something of a quiet character, but since the departure of his wife, his reticence is said to have become something akin to taciturn surliness."

"Perhaps that is no more than simple gossip, Papa?"

"Perhaps it is, my child, but it seems to be an opinion firmly held by a number of people I would consider to be somewhat more reliable in their recitation."

"And do they say the circumstances in which the Earl's wife departed?" In truth, Mary did not consider herself to be a gossip, and she most certainly did not enjoy to hear whispered tales of other people's lives. However, on this occasion, she rather felt that it might be more helpful to know the circumstances in case it would happen to assist her in the teaching and raising of two four-year-old children.

"There is not *one* who has any notion of the circumstances, Mary. The woman seems simply to have vanished, and beyond the fact that she has gone, the Earl has spoken nothing of it. Even the gossips can say nothing of any prior scandal or rumor surrounding the couple. That is just another thing, my dear." William Porter's eyebrows had knitted together in a concerned frown as he watched his daughter pour boiling water over the tea leaves. "Is it really sensible to go into a home where something rather significant has occurred but of which you have no detail?"

"In truth, Papa, I cannot see what the business has to do with me. I should have liked to have known purely because it is undoubtedly a question which shall affect my two charges, but beyond that, I have very little interest in the matter."

"And I believe you, Mary. You never really were one for gossip, were you?" William smiled warmly at his daughter.

"No, Papa, I truthfully never have been interested in gossip."

Mary carried the large teapot to the table and set it down in the middle. Opening the large dresser, she took down two tea cups and saucers and set those upon the table also. She sat down again and smiled over at her father, leaving the tea to brew for a little while longer before pouring.

"I must say, I'm rather surprised at an Earl employing such a wealthy woman to act as governess to his children," William said, his eyes resting vaguely upon the teapot.

"Really? Why so?"

"Well, much apart from it being far from the ordinary way of things, I should imagine that he would find the employment of a wealthy young woman to be potentially quite temporary."

"You mean because I have money, I could decide upon a whim that I no longer wanted to work, and would leave the children?"

"Quite so, my dear."

"Yes, I rather thought the same as you, Papa," Mary said, her cheeks flushing inexplicably.

"But presumably, the Earl of Pennington had no such reservation?" William Porter knew his child of old, and the flush on her cheeks spoke volumes to him.

"I did not see any reason to mention my wealth, Papa. The Earl is entirely unaware of it, and presumably, thinks that he is employing a governess who very much needs the work rather than one who wants the work."

"Are you sure that's wise, Mary?"

"I can see no reason for the Earl of Pennington to be made aware of my private financial circumstances." Her shoulders stiffened, and she raised her head just a little. "I shall be undertaking the work most seriously, and have no intention of quitting it to simply rely upon my wealth. In truth, I'm sure that I shall give the Earl no need to regret appointing me."

"No, indeed I'm sure you will not my dear. My only concern is that, should he find it out in some other way... I would... well, might he not then dismiss you?"

"I suppose that is a possibility, Papa. However, if I'm doing a good job, then to dismiss me would surely be a foolish act. And again, if he does dismiss me, it is not as though I shall be without money, is it?"

"No, indeed you shall not." William smiled a little. "You know, my dear, I quite often forget that we are wealthy. At the back of my mind, there always lurks that tiny fear of loss of employment and other such similar things. Silly, isn't it?"

"No, Papa. It is not silly... it is simply a habit. And beyond that, it speaks of how well you respect your new fortune and how grateful you are for it. Many other men in your position would have developed the customary air of entitlement, and yet you have avoided that. No, indeed, Papa. There is nothing silly in what you say."

Mary rose from the table again and kissed her father lightly on the top of his head before pouring the tea. As they both settled to drinking the hot and nicely brewed infusion, Mary had to blink hard for a few moments to stay the tears which had rather surprised her. The cozy and happy familiarity of their early morning ritual around the kitchen table felt suddenly like the safest place on earth. Like the place, she most wanted to be. Mary knew that it was simply nerves and sadness at the thought of leaving, and she most certainly knew that she was strong enough to take on any challenge which came her way. However, at that moment, she felt like a child of eight staring up at her beloved Papa and wishing that life would never have to change.

"Well, my dear, it seems to me as if you have thought it all through and have very much made up your mind. So, now that I've done my very best to dissuade you, and failed miserably, when does your employment begin?" William gave a teasing smile which Mary knew very well.

"It is but three weeks from now, Papa." Mary hurriedly dashed a tiny tear from the corner of her eye, knowing full well that her father was very sensible of it. "And in any case, I shall barely be outside of Denmouth, and I shall see you some Sundays." Mary seemed to be comforting herself as much as she was trying to comfort her father.

"Very true, Mary. Linwood is as close to Denmouth as Denmouth is itself," William said with a hearty laugh designed to raise his daughter's spirits.

"Oh, Papa! How I shall miss you!"

"And I shall miss you too, my sweet child."

As Mary sipped on her tea, she wondered if life would ever be the same again.

CHAPTER 2

*E*merson Rutherford, the Earl of Pennington, watched from the window of his study as the new governess climbed down from the carriage. The driver lifted one and then another rather large trunk from the back, and left them on the gravel driveway for the footman to carry into the house. Emerson's forehead wrinkled in vague interest as he wondered at the amount of her belongings. In truth, he could never have packed his own belongings given one hundred or two hundred such trunks, yet the woman below seemed to be arriving with very much more than any other member of his staff had done before. He sighed and shook his head; surely this was of little interest to him.

Mary Porter seemed to have a confidence of bearing that he had not entirely been expecting when he had interviewed her for the post. Of the seven candidates, five had been sent to him from an employment registry, and only Mary and one other had applied in their own right in answer to the newspaper advertisement he had placed. In truth, he had almost left the choice down to the employment agency themselves, little wanting to spend any time meeting and interviewing a host of women. However, common sense had prevailed in the end, and he had decided to take an active part in deciding who should help to raise Oliver and Isobel.

If he was honest, Emerson was rather glad that he had given himself the final say in the choice of a governess, for Mary Porter had proved to be rather exceptional in comparison with the other six candidates. There had been nothing wrong with the remainder, simply that none of them had the same air of intelligence and efficiency which Miss Porter had displayed. She had a certain forthrightness of manner which he deduced might come in very handy in raising four-year-old twins who had been giving their nurse a certain amount of anguish for the full twelve months since their mother had left.

Something about Mary Porter had given Emerson the distinct feeling that she would be more than a match for Oliver and Isobel.

Emerson had been about to turn from the window when something seemed to catch his eye. As the footman walked away into the house carrying her luggage, and the carriage driver regained his seat and made to drive away, Mary Porter seemed to stand in absolute stillness, completely alone on the driveway for just a few moments.

Emerson drew closer to the window as if to see better. Mary turned and looked out across the lawns of his immaculate estate, seemingly to the countryside beyond. There was something in her manner which he could not discern, and yet he found that he wanted to. Whatever it was, he did not believe it to be nerves, for she had shown no sign of such in the brief time in which she was in his company. Rather there seemed to be something almost melancholy in her stance, although she was most upright in her posture and without any hint of the stoop which would ordinarily give away a sadness of some kind. All in all, he quite simply could not fathom it. Shiny brown hair curled from beneath her bonnet and quite unfashionably, there was the hint of a tan on her skin. Then he realized, this was not a woman of wealth and leisure. She would have to work outside no matter what the weather so the color was not unsurprising. As he stared, she moved and in no time at all she had turned back to face the building. After briefly smoothing her skirts and raising her hands to check her hair, Mary Porter strode purposefully into the house and out of his view.

"How nice to see you again, Miss Porter. I trust your journey went well?" Jean Miller, the housekeeper, was a sturdy and efficient woman of around fifty years of age. Mary had met her on the day of her interview with the Earl and had found her a most agreeable woman.

"I thank you, Mrs. Miller, it did indeed. In truth, it was rather a short journey." Mary returned the smile, although she had to admit to some small fluttering of nerves in her belly.

"Oh, of course!" Mrs. Miller chuckled. "Well, I daresay that the journey from Denmouth is but a matter of twenty minutes, is it not?"

"Indeed, you are right, Mrs. Miller." Mary looked all about her. They were standing in the large kitchen of Linwood Hall, and Mary fully appreciated the complete sense of order that was to be found there. The kitchen and the rooms around it seemed to be a hive of activity, and very much the heart of the servants' operations. Mary could hear much cheerful banter and conversation being passed between the servants and felt warmed by what she thought to be a great sense of camaraderie. She wondered if she soon might become a part of it. In truth, Mary knew that her own accommodations would be within the greater part of the house, very much nearer to the children's rooms than the servants' quarters, but still she relished the idea of finding friends amongst the rest of the staff.

"Are you nervous, Miss Porter?" Mrs. Miller had a lovely round face which wrinkled pleasingly as she smiled, turning her dark eyes into small, shiny currants.

"In truth, I do believe I am, Mrs. Miller. I really hadn't thought about it until I arrived upon the driveway. It was there where my nerves finally caught up with me, I think." Mary gave a light and tinkling laugh, and could hardly recognize it as her own. Right up until the very last moment, Mary had never once expected to feel nervous, and the feeling had rather taken her by surprise.

"Well, don't you worry about a thing, Miss Porter. We shall consider looking after you a treat, and you'll settle in in no time." Jean Miller reached out and lightly patted Mary's upper arm reassuringly. "Why don't I get you nice and settled in? Your packing trunks have already been sent to your room, so I'll take you there now and show you around a little bit so that you can get your bearings. And once we've done that, we'll come back here and have a nice cup of tea."

Mrs. Miller bustled away, and Mary hurriedly followed in her wake. She was glad for a few moments walking since the older woman's kindly welcome had made her feel a little tearful. All in all, this little rush of emotion was not something which Mary ordinarily had to deal with, and she was finding it rather disconcerting.

Mary was surprised to find that her rooms really were in the heart of Linwood Hall, and very much where the rest of the family rooms were. Mrs. Miller ushered her into a large and very pretty bedroom. There was a double bed with rather plentiful and pretty linens and an overall brightness about the room which Mary could only attribute to the size of the windows.

Hurrying over to the windows, Mary looked out hungrily upon the beautiful and immaculate grounds of Linwood Hall. Not for one moment had she expected to have such a room, and with such a view!

"Lovely, isn't it?" Mrs. Miller said, brightly. Mary hardly knew what to say, rather feeling that the housekeeper's rooms would be nowhere near as large and as nicely decorated as her own.

"It really is, Mrs. Miller. In truth, I had not expected it to be quite so large and pretty." Mary felt a stab of discomfort and hoped that the differences in accommodations between herself and the other staff would not draw a line between them. Of course, in most houses, the governess was always a little apart from the servants, but Mary had rather hoped to be not *quite* so distant. Still, Mrs. Miller seemed not to be at all put out by it, rather, she seemed genuinely pleased to be showing Mary around such pretty quarters.

"Mrs. Miller, have the children had a governess before?" Mary did not quite know where the question had come from, and yet somehow it seemed vital that it be answered.

"No indeed, Miss Porter, you shall be the first. They have a nurse, of course, and she has looked after them since they were babies. But, in truth, they have become a little much for her, and she's starting to look towards her own retirement.

15

The Earl would always have brought in a governess anyway, for the teaching of them, but I think that he has chosen to take on a governess sooner rather than later to relieve some of the burden from Miss Morgan."

"And is Miss Morgan so close to retirement?" Mary was suddenly gripped by a small amount of panic; was she really ready to take on every aspect of care for the two children?

"Well, no. I daresay that Miss Morgan shall remain here another two or three years, my dear, but she shall be much better off for being only responsible for getting the children ready in the morning, and getting them to bed at night. I think the days were growing too long for her, and the Earl could see that if he did not get some help for her soon, he would simply be hastening her departure."

"Are the children really such a handful?" Mary tried as best she could to make her voice matter of fact. She was very well aware that, in the interview, the notion of dealing with two children who might well be a little challenging was something that she had claimed would be of little issue to her. As she spoke to Mrs. Miller, Mary did not want to give away the idea that she had been employed in error.

"Well, Miss Morgan says that they can be a little high-spirited and awkward from time to time if I'm completely honest. They very likely are a challenge, and yet I cannot help but feel sorry for the little mites. They were barely talking, you see, when their mother went away, and I still think that they struggle to understand why it is that she is no longer here. And you know these aristocratic families, Miss Porter, nobody ever says what it is that is really troubling them. I think the children might misbehave at times as a way of trying to understand the world around them, and why it changed so greatly." Mrs. Miller smiled so warmly as she stared off into the distance, that Mary felt she could truly perceive a great love for the two little children. The idea of them suddenly becoming motherless did something to Mary's resolve, and she felt rather more determined to rise to the challenge than she had in the previous moments. All in all, Mary decided to put her reservations down to nothing more than simple nerves and regained something of her old confidence in her own abilities.

Despite the fact that she truly was not a gossip of any kind, Mary had to fight hard against the urge to ask Mrs. Miller where exactly it was that the children's mother had gone. She felt sure that the dear woman would have told her, but Mary felt that it was a subject which she should steer clear of for just a while longer. After all, Mary could always ask Mrs. Miller at a later date, and likely be assured of an answer. In the meantime, she would simply have to wonder.

"That sounds like a terrible shame for them, Mrs. Miller." Mary smiled and inclined her head sadly. "And what of the Earl himself? How do you find him as an employer, if you don't mind me asking, Mrs. Miller?" Mary rather finished the question with far less confidence than she had started it with. Perhaps Mrs. Miller would not take kindly to being asked to pass comment upon the Earl of Pennington by a woman who had literally just walked into Linwood Hall. Mary could feel her cheeks flush a little, and very much wished that she had not spoken.

"Oh, he's a good and fair employer, in all honesty. He's certainly not the friendliest of people, but even *that* has not always been so." Mrs. Miller chewed her bottom lip in reminiscence. Mary found great comfort in the fact that the housekeeper had not been at all antagonized by the question. "I've worked here for many years, Miss Porter... ever since my husband died in fact." Mrs. Miller was staring off into the distance, clearly trying to count the number of years since the passing of her husband. "Goodness me, it must be almost fifteen years now! Anyway, I have worked here in all that time and never found the Earl to cause me any problems. As long as the house is running smoothly, he more or less allows us all to just get on with it. He's always been a quiet sort of a man, and that I've never minded myself. I must admit, though, he has his sour moments these days. Still, I'm sure there's none can blame him for that in light of all that happened." Mrs. Miller finished with an air of magnanimity. Mary very much gathered that Mrs. Miller was under the impression that she knew more about the circumstances surrounding the departure of the Earl's wife than she really did.

"Oh, I'm sure." Mary tactfully left it at that.

"Now then, perhaps you ought to unpack and hang your dresses before we go and have tea? That way the creases shall fall out of them sooner."

"Oh yes, of course, Mrs. Miller. Really, how kind you are." Once again Mary was assailed by a vaguely tearful feeling.

"It's nothing, my dear. And I should be very glad to stay and help if you'd like me to."

"Thank you, Mrs. Miller. I should very much like you to stay with me whilst I unpack." Mary began to unlock the lids of the trunks. In truth, she really *did* want Mrs. Miller to stay with her. Mary had a sneaking suspicion that, should she be left for ten minutes alone, she might very well give in to the strange emotions which had been swirling all about her from the moment she had arrived.

CHAPTER 3

*M*ary felt somewhat nervous as she made her way to the drawing room later that day. Mrs. Miller had shown her around quite thoroughly, and already Mary felt that she was coming to know the layout of Linwood Hall. Mary had still not met Oliver and Isobel, despite having arrived in the mid-morning, and she found she was growing a little anxious about it. As nice as it had been to come to know her way around so quickly, Mary could not help but feel that meeting the children would have somehow settled her down a little. Not to mention the fact that she had not seen or heard anything of the Earl from the moment she had arrived. The ridiculous thought that he was avoiding her had occurred to Mary, but she dismissed it out of hand.

It was almost four o'clock in the afternoon before she had finally been summoned to the drawing room to reacquaint herself with the Earl of Pennington and to meet his children for the first time. Of course, by that time, Mrs. Miller had a myriad of other duties to attend to, many of which she had been putting off for the entire afternoon she had spent with Mary. Although Mary had assured the good and kind housekeeper that she could most certainly find her own way to the drawing room now, in her heart, she wished she did not have to enter alone. Silently chiding herself for this sudden nervousness and seeming weakness of nature, Mary took a deep breath, straightened her spine, and strode with purpose in the direction of the drawing room.

Once there, Mary knocked briskly, pushing the door open almost immediately and walked in. Never having been in service, and not particularly classing herself as a servant as such, Mary had no intention of hovering and quivering on the other side of the door waiting for an instruction to enter. After all, had she not been sent for?

"Come…" The Earl had clearly been about to instruct her to come in but was stopped in his tracks when she quite suddenly appeared before him. "Oh."

"Lord Pennington," Mary said in as a steady a voice as she could manage as she dropped the smallest of curtsies.

"Well, yes, Miss Porter." For a moment, it seemed as if the Earl could not quite think of how to open the conversation. The Earl had not been sitting when she arrived but had been standing looking out of one of the large windows, seemingly across at the rolling green hills of the surrounding countryside. He seemed to look about him as if wondering where might be the best place for them to sit whilst they conducted this initial bit of business. Perhaps he had not been expecting her to arrive quite so promptly, but Mary felt she could hardly be blamed for efficiency.

Mary's eyes scoured the room, clearly perplexed as to why the children were not yet with him. Surely the time for her to meet them had come. It seemed to Mary that, since she had been there all day without meeting them, the idea that they were somewhat troubled and their behavior might well be a little challenging had rather grown out of all proportion in her mind. The mixture of nerves and her bemusement at the content of her first day at Linwood Hall had rather got the better of her, and she knew it.

Whilst Mary had run her Dame school from the drawing room of her own home in Denmouth, she had been entirely in charge. In fact, Mary had never worked for anybody before and, as she stood before the Earl of Pennington, she realized that she had not considered how very different an experience it might be. Certainly, teaching was teaching, no matter where it took place. However, actually being employed was going to be a very different experience for Mary, and she did not yet know if it was an experience for the better. Seeing her look around, the Earl had clearly gathered that she was looking for the children.

"Ah, yes, the children. Their nurse, Miss Morgan, should be bringing them along any moment. In fact, I rather expected that she might be here by now." Finally, the Earl moved from his statue-like position in the window. He walked around the back of an extremely long and heavily brocaded couch and, reaching its edge, indicated with a vague sweep of his hand that Mary should take a seat upon it. The Earl himself sat down on a high wingback chair of the same heavy material opposite her.

"Thank you, Lord Pennington," Mary said as she took her seat.

"I trust Mrs. Miller has shown you around and that you are well settled in your quarters?" The Earl spoke as if he really and truly had very little interest whatsoever in hearing her answer. In truth, it seemed to Mary as if he was simply filling time before Miss Morgan arrived with Oliver and Isobel.

"Indeed, Lord Pennington. Mrs. Miller has been extremely helpful, and I am very well settled. I thank you, Sir." As much as Mary tried to address the Earl in her speech, she was rather disconcerted by his determined gaze at a point on the back of the couch just to the right of her.

It took an effort of will for Mary to not actually turn in her seat and look to see what it was he was looking at. However, Mary was a sharp and intelligent woman and was very sensible of the fact that his addressing the back of the couch was simply a way of not having to engage with her entirely. She took a few moments to try to discern whether his behavior was a lack of confidence, a lack of interest, or blatant rudeness. Since he was the Earl and she was merely the governess, Mary knew very well that the answer to that question would be of little matter in the end. After all, she could hardly tackle him on the state of his manners as she might have done one of the pupils at her Dame school.

"Good. Well, good," the Earl said to the back of the couch.

In the moments that he continued to study the heavy brocade, Mary chose to study the Earl. That he was extremely tall, she had perceived in their initial meeting, but she had rather forgotten it until she saw him standing in the window as she had entered the drawing room. His light brown hair was flecked with dashes of blond here and there and, coupled with the light tan of his skin, Mary quickly ascertained that the Earl must be something of an outdoor man. In truth, she rather liked that about him, if nothing else as yet. The current fashion for rather willowy and pale-looking men, particularly aristocrats, was something that Mary had never fully understood. As much as she had declared herself to be little interested in romance, Mary still thought that a man ought to look like a man. The Earl of Pennington most certainly, in Mary's opinion, looked like a man.

He was neatly dressed in dark, fawn-colored breeches and a waistcoat of the same color over a white shirt with full and flowing billowy sleeves. The cuffs were neatly held together at the wrist by small and neat silver cufflinks, and the cravat of his shirt had been knotted to perfection. His long black boots were immaculately clean, with cuffs in a deep tan leather. And yet somehow, despite the neatness of his apparel, Mary thought she could perceive something less than neat about the man himself. The very thought gave her a most curious feeling, and she could not begin to imagine why she had formulated such an opinion. In truth, she could not imagine that the Earl of Pennington was in any way a wild sort of man, and yet still the feeling persisted. The feeling that beneath the starched appearance and the even stiffer manner, there was a very different man trying to escape.

Mary could feel her cheeks warming a little, and hoped that she was not blushing. Quite why she had thought such a thing, she could not account for.

Allowing her gaze to rest upon his face, since he still appeared to be looking anywhere but at her, Mary realized that he was actually a very handsome man. His eyes were a light and attractive blue and looked very well against his tanned and smooth skin. Quite what sort of teeth he had, Mary could not say, for she had yet to see the man smile.

Perhaps perceiving himself to be the subject of her scrutiny, the Earl tore his gaze from the back of the couch and rested his eyes firmly upon Mary's. The move had been so subtle and yet so sudden that she had almost gasped, and she knew very well that there would be no denying the blush on her cheeks now. Without really knowing what she should say, Mary opened her mouth as if to speak. Fortunately for her, at that very moment, there was a clattering and chattering outside the drawing room door, coupled with the harsh tones of a clearly beleaguered nurse trying to quiet down her charges before presenting them to their father.

"Now, you mind my words, Oliver. I shall not tell you again!" The hurried sentence came out in something of a rather loud stage whisper, and for an awful moment, Mary thought she might laugh.

"Do come in, Miss Morgan," the Earl said with barely disguised exasperation before the nurse had even got as far as knocking upon the door.

Mary turned her head just enough to see a woman in her mid-fifties bustling into the room in a somewhat stooped fashion. Initially thinking that the woman must have a complaint of some sort, Mary quickly realized that she was having to bend down slightly to take the hands of the little boy and girl on either side of her. Whilst the woman was indeed tall, it rather struck Mary that the children themselves seemed awfully small for their age. Mary had taught quite a variety of children in her tiny school and was perfectly well aware of the average size and shape of a four-year-old. Neither of the two children wandering into the room and gently squirming in order to seek release from their nurse fitted that particular standard.

As Miss Morgan drew them further into the room, Mary could see that both of the children had inherited their father's blond hair, although, in their youth, it was very much paler than his own. They had also inherited his blue eyes and, against the pale hair and pale faces, these eyes made them look almost angelic. However, the harried expression on the face of the aging nurse rather told its own story in that regard.

"Well, children, have you been good today?" The Earl seemed to address his small children with the same lack of interest with which he had addressed Mary herself. Mary looked from the awkward little faces back to the Earl's. He himself looked rather a mixture of stern fortitude and exasperation, and Mary could not begin to imagine how that briefest presence of his own children had engendered such a look.

Something about the look on his face and the way he had spoken to the children made Mary feel a little angry. Casting her mind back, she could never remember a time when her own father had addressed her in such a manner. William Porter had always been the most loving and interested of fathers, and she entirely attributed her intelligence and confidence to his lifelong devotion to his children. Indeed, her father had never once shown the look of exasperation which the Earl had worn, and yet, after the death of her mother, William Porter had raised his four children with very little outside help. Mary had to stop herself from rising to her feet and demanding to know why a man who seemingly had very little to do with the day-to-day upbringing of his own children thought he had the right to look so very put upon by their mere presence.

Once again, Mary was reminded that having an actual employer carried with it the pitfall of having to keep one's opinions very much to oneself.

"Yes, Papa," chimed the two little angel faces in perfect unison.

"Miss Morgan?" The Earl cast his eyes upwards towards the nurse, presumably for confirmation.

"Not entirely, My Lord. Still, I daresay they tried their best," Miss Morgan replied.

Mary had been all set to feel rather sorry for this aging nurse. From what Mrs. Miller had told her, the woman was beginning to feel rather tired by life. A situation which had not been improved by the behavior of the children. Even as she had heard the woman outside the door, seemingly desperately trying to ensure that her charges behaved, at least for the next ten minutes, still Mary had rather felt something for her. However, something about the coolness of the woman's response, and her rather sarcastic suggestion that the two tiny children had *tried their best*, had almost entirely turned Mary's feeling about her upon its head.

That one sentence had struck Mary as a rather unnecessary attempt to show the two little children in a poor light in their father's eyes. It was Mary's view that, if the children had indeed been misbehaving all day, then at least part of the fault must lie with the woman who had acted as their nurse for their entire lives. For who would know them better than she? In aristocratic homes, Mary rather believed it was common for nurses and governesses to have far stronger emotional ties to their charges than their own parents did.

Once again Mary found herself biting her tongue. In her heart, she wanted to tell the woman that keeping such negative feelings to herself at that moment would have done much to engender the goodwill, not to mention good behavior, of the children in the future. After all, if she seemed to stand up for them in the face of a rather stern father, the children would have a greater feeling for her, and perhaps not misbehave for her in the future.

Although Mary had had much experience with young children, she knew that they were very much less complicated than many people imagined them to be. Loving kindness and a little bit of loyalty went a very long way with a small child if adults did but know it.

Not wanting the critical conversation to continue any further, Mary rather shifted in her seat in such a way as to draw attention to herself. The Earl seemed to suddenly remember her presence, not to mention the reason for her being there and, to Mary's relief, he set about the introductions.

"Now then, children, this young lady here is to be your governess. Her name is Miss Porter," he said, in rather matter-of-fact tones.

Judging by the way the children looked so curiously at her, Mary rather wondered if this was the first they had heard of it. Perhaps the Earl and this rather doughy and red-faced nurse had not thought any prior explanation to Oliver and Isobel was in any way warranted.

Although so few sentences had passed since the nurse and the children had entered the room, Mary could almost feel that she could not stand any more of it.

"It's very nice to meet you, Oliver and Isobel. As your father said, I am to be your new governess. That means that I'm going to start to teach you some new and very interesting things. I hope we shall have a very nice time together." Mary had swiveled in her seat to entirely face the children and smiled warmly at each of the pale blank faces. Both children blinked at her with a mixture of shyness and curiosity, but neither one of them spoke. Mary did not know if it was simply because they did not know what to say, or if they were not accustomed to being allowed to speak in front of their father unless responding to a direct question.

"Do you both like stories?" Mary went on, determined to have some response or other out of them. If she were to be their governess, and have the teaching of them, then she would most certainly do things her way. Mary looked at both of the children and gave them what she very much hoped was her warmest smile.

"Yes, Miss Porter." Oliver was the first to speak. His voice was so tiny and reedy that she barely heard him.

"Well, I'm glad to hear it, Oliver, for I have many, *many* exciting stories to tell you." Mary smiled at him and was gratified to see his pale little face become suddenly mobile, and the first crease of a smile began to form. "And what of, Isobel? Should *you* like to hear some of my exciting stories?"

"I like stories, Miss Porter," Isobel said, before dropping her shy gaze to the floor. When Mary saw the tiny white cheeks suddenly flush pink, she could have leaped to her feet and scooped the little girl into her arms.

"Well then, I promise you both that we shall start our very first day together with a story. As soon as we have had our breakfast and we are in the schoolroom, I shall tell you one of my very most favorite stories, and that shall start our day."

Oliver and Isobel surreptitiously looked at each other, and Mary rather thought she could sense a little frisson of excitement.

"Well, children, I'm sure it's been very nice for you to meet Miss Porter tonight, and you shall see her again in the morning. Please see that you behave yourselves whilst Miss Morgan gives you your meal and puts you to bed this evening." The Earl's austere tone had not changed, and Mary felt a very sudden and intense dislike for the man.

"Thank you, Miss Morgan." The Earl nodded at the nurse, clearly indicating that she could leave with the children.

Mary also shifted to the very edge of the couch, hopeful that she was indicating her intention to leave also. However, she was very sensible of the fact that she was in the presence of an Earl of the Realm, and would very much have to wait to be *dismissed*.

"The children seem to have taken to you very well, Miss Porter." The Earl began.

"Thank you, Your Lordship," Mary said, hoping that he would not perceive the flatness in her voice.

"The nurse tells me that they are often very challenging, as indeed I believe I told you upon interview. I understand the very real needs to befriend children in your care, to a certain extent. However, I should very much rather they are not indulged in any kind of bad behavior."

Mary did everything in her power to hide how she felt about his deep and unjustified insult.

"Indeed, Your Lordship." Once again, Mary found herself having to bite her own tongue, quite literally.

"Well, thank you, Miss Porter." The Earl nodded in the same perfunctory way as he had to the nurse. Mary understood very well that he was dismissing her also, and found that she was only too glad to accede to his request.

Mary made her way rather smartly to the library, rightly judging that it would most likely be empty. Once inside, she took several deep breaths in order to calm her anger. What a terrible and insufferable man the Earl of Pennington truly was!

Almost unavoidably, Mary thought of the personal wealth which had rendered her entirely independent. In as much as the notion had settled her nerves and provided her with a certain sense of security, Mary could not help but think of the two tiny pale faces, and the blue eyes with which they had regarded her so shyly.

Although she knew she might have the situation entirely wrong, given that she had only been in the family's company, but a few short minutes, Mary was almost overwhelmed with the determination to ensure that the two small four-year-olds should soon come to know her as a friend and an ally.

As much as she had nodded and smiled politely at the Earl, Mary had decided that she really would do things her own way.

CHAPTER 4

*M*ary had slept rather fitfully. Rising at seven o'clock, she threw open the window of her bedroom and took in several deep breaths of the sharp early morning air. Feeling somewhat more revived, Mary hurriedly washed and dressed before making her way down to the servants' quarters.

She knew that the children were now to start taking their breakfast with her instead of the nurse and that they would be doing so at half past eight. That gave her over an hour to spare, and her afternoon spent with Mrs. Miller had furnished Mary with much information of the housekeeper's general movements. In truth, she found herself rather hoping that there would be time for the two women to at least have a cup of tea together.

As she reached the kitchen, Mary could see that all of the servants seemed to be busy, either with tasks or the preparation of tasks. While she received many polite nods, and *good mornings*, for the most part, they all seemed too busy to dare to stop and ask if she needed anything.

It was with some relief, therefore, that she spied Mrs. Miller walking smartly down the long corridor which ran adjacent to the kitchen. Feeling a little foolish, she spun on her heel and darted out of the kitchen, her smart boots clipping noisily on the flagstones as she went.

"Good morning, Mrs. Miller," Mary said, quite breathless.

"Why, good morning, Miss Porter. Did you sleep well?" The fact that Mrs. Miller did not seem at all perturbed to see the new governess in the servants' quarters, made Mary feel very much less self-conscious.

"In truth, Mrs. Miller, I did not." Mary could hardly believe she had been so embarrassingly honest. "But I daresay it is simply my new surroundings."

"Oh, yes, my dear, a new bed, and a new room can be most disconcerting. Come along, shall we have a nice pot of tea to start the day?" Mrs. Miller's bright smile dissolved Mary's embarrassment in a heartbeat. Mary quite rightly perceived that the housekeeper knew very well that the new governess was yet to be relaxed within the walls of Linwood Hall, and that she had sought out the one person she felt comfortable with at the earliest opportunity. It was a need that Mary had never experienced before, and she was tremendously grateful that Mrs. Miller seemed very sensible of it without actually alluding to it.

"Oh, yes, please. I should be most terribly grateful, Mrs. Miller."

After asking one of the kitchen maids to prepare a tea tray, Mrs. Miller gently ushered Mary into what appeared to be her own little office. Because of the woman's warmth and kindness, it had completely escaped Mary's mind that Mrs. Miller, as housekeeper, would rank rather highly amongst the rest of the staff. In fact, it was undoubtedly true that she was second only to the Butler in that vast world below stairs. That the woman had her own office and could lightly command a kitchen maid to bring in some tea should not, in truth, have surprised Mary. And yet somehow, it did. However, Mary was gratified to note that Mrs. Miller had asked the young girl to prepare the tea in a most kind and respectful manner; something more akin to asking a favor than issuing an order.

Once the young girl had brought the tray in and rested it upon the table, Mrs. Miller thanked her kindly, and the girl left.

"Now then, what is troubling you, Miss Porter?" Mrs. Miller asked kindly as she set about pouring two cups of tea.

"Oh dear me, am I so obvious?" Mary laughed a little nervously before continuing. "Mrs. Miller, I know it is probably just a case of my getting used to things here, but I rather found myself feeling a little uneasy in the company of the Earl. Not that he did or said anything which could possibly have upset me, in truth. Rather, it is the way that he conversed with his children." Mary faltered slightly, not really knowing how to proceed. After all, Mrs. Miller had been the housekeeper at Linwood Hall for many years and undoubtedly held her employer in high regard. "Oh, I don't know, Mrs. Miller. He just seems so cold with them, so austere. And they really are so *dreadfully tiny*."

With a certain amount of horror, Mary realized that her eyes were beginning to brim with hot tears. She quite successfully blinked them away without them falling, and yet knew that they had been very obvious to Mrs. Miller.

"Yes, I do believe I have felt very much the same as you do

about that particular relationship. The sad thing is, it has not always been so." The light pat on the hand which Mrs. Miller gave Mary reassured her more than anything that the woman could have said.

"Has it not?" Mary said, her voice almost a whisper.

"No, it hasn't. As cold as the Earl might seem now, he has not always been this way. It is true to say that he has suffered greatly, this last year," Mrs. Miller began. "And I truly believe that his children have also suffered, which is likely to explain the reports of poor behavior. The sad thing is that it is reports of this behavior which seems to be driving some sort of wedge between the Earl and the twins."

"But really, can their behavior be *so* terrible?"

"I believe that the children have rather made Miss Morgan's life something of a trial to her of late. In some ways, it is this that has edged her towards thoughts of early retirement. Miss Morgan tells me that their father has spoken to them on a number of occasions in a bid to improve things, but seemingly it has had little effect."

"Do forgive me if you have already told me this, but has Miss Morgan been their nurse for their entire lives?" Mary tried to make the question sound as if it was asked without any judgment whatsoever. She had no idea how close the housekeeper and nurse were, particularly since they had both worked in the Earl's home for a number of years. Mary had the most dreadful feeling of needing to walk on egg shells; she did not want to do anything to alienate her one and only ally.

"Yes, she has been here from the very first. In fact, she was already in residence before the twins were born."

"Indeed? I must say, that seems rather unusual." Mary was pleased to note that her voice had lost some of its timidity as her interest was suddenly piqued.

"Perhaps not as unusual as it might seem. You see, Miss Morgan had been Lady Pennington's *own* nurse, and she had brought her with her to Linwood when she married the Earl."

"Oh, I see." Mary could think of several questions she was desperate to ask, but rather feared showing herself up as a determined gossip.

"Still, it was almost three years before the Earl and Countess conceived the twins, so Miss Morgan was rather more of a companion to Lady Pennington if you will. It seemed to be the only occupation she could sensibly be offered until the appearance of children in the home."

"Oh, yes, of course. Well, that makes sense." Mary really did not know what else to say. With her questions burning brightly in her brain, Mary fought to think of something bland and innocuous. "Oh, well, Miss Morgan really must be dreadfully fond of the twins." Mary smiled sweetly, despite a certain feeling of distaste that she could not shed as she thought of the aging and rotund nurse. "Even if they do rather challenge her with their behavior."

"I assume she does, rather than knowing it for certain. You see, Miss Morgan speaks to me but rarely. I daresay that, having arrived at Linwood as a companion, she is rather more comfortable above stairs than below them." Although her words made her feelings rather clear, Mrs. Miller did not speak them with a tone of malice. Rather it seemed to Mary more of a simple observation than a judgment.

"Oh, well, I can already attest to the fact that Miss Morgan is missing out by maintaining her segregation," Mary spoke completely genuinely and was rewarded with a warm and gratified smile from her companion.

"What a lovely thing to say, Miss Porter."

"Oh, please believe me when I tell you that I mean it, Mrs. Miller. You have truly made me feel welcome here, so much so that here I am seeking you out at barely seven o'clock in the morning for a cup of tea and some conversation." Mary laughed.

"And I'm glad you did, Miss Porter."

"I suppose Miss Morgan found it rather upsetting when Lady Pennington left? After all, having been her nurse, surely she had known the lady all her life."

"Oh, I rather think that she was most upset, for I do not think she expected for a moment that the Countess would leave her behind," Mrs. Miller said, in a low and somewhat conspiratorial whisper.

"Indeed?" Mary knew that she was teetering upon the brink of nosiness, and yet she was suddenly rather intrigued by it all.

"Well, of course, it was all so sudden, but I really cannot think that leaving Miss Morgan behind was a simple oversight on the part of the Lady Pennington." Mrs. Miller took a long sip of her tea as she stared thoughtfully into space. "No, I cannot think that leaving Miss Morgan behind was anything other than purposeful."

"Did the Countess leave of her own accord?" Finally, Mary broke her cardinal rule and was about to indulge in gossip. However, it was clear to Mary that Mrs. Miller rather assumed her to have more knowledge of the situation than she actually did. Perhaps it was only right to set things straight in that regard.

"Oh, yes, Miss Porter, Lady Pennington *chose* to leave Linwood Hall and everyone in it far behind her."

"Including her children," Mary said, sadly.

"Yes, that's the saddest of all, isn't it?"

"Yes, Mrs. Miller, *it is* the saddest of all."

"It caused something of a scandal at the time, of course, but it was more or less contained within Linwood Hall. You see, the Earl was not a tremendous socializer in the first place, and so he did not have a wide circle of friends, or so-called friends, who could spread the details of what had happened far and wide. Add to that the fact that he became so very severe after it had happened, it is easy to see how disinclined the staff and servants are to discuss the matter outside of the estate. So, there really were no outsiders particularly who witnessed the fast-growing friendship between Lady Pennington and Count Ettore Costanzo, and therefore there were none to really suspect *where* she had gone and *with whom* by the time she had departed."

"A Count? Italian, presumably?" It was all Mary could do to stop her eyes widening and her mouth drooping open. That the Earl of Pennington's wife had run away with a foreign Count was absolutely the last thing she had been expecting. In truth, Mary had rather wondered if the Countess of Pennington had lost her reason and been sent to an asylum. That was all she could think of which would account for the lack of public knowledge and the Earl's surly countenance. As Mary sat drinking her tea in astonishment, she rather wondered at herself and the ridiculousness of her curious supposition. Perhaps she really *did* read too many books.

"Yes, Miss Porter, he was Italian. But he wasn't just *any* Italian count... Count Ettore Costanzo is a relative of the Earl's. He is a cousin of some sort, albeit I believe a rather distant one. Anyway, the Count was staying here at Linwood Hall on his very first trip to England. And presumably his last, for when he left, he left with his cousin's wife."

"But surely the Earl had seen it coming?" Mary gave up all pretense of being a sanctimonious decrier of gossip.

"I truly think that he did not see it coming. And in any household, the servants are always around and often the first to pick up on any little intrigues that occur within its walls. Yet, truly, everybody here was in amazement when Lady Pennington and the Count disappeared. Or, *nearly* everybody." Mrs. Miller added the last with a little flush to her cheeks. Mary rather gathered that whatever came next would be an absolute secret.

"Nearly everybody?" Mary leaned in towards Mrs. Miller, keen to inspire trust in the woman.

"Well, I've never really spoken of this before, but on the day that Lady Pennington disappeared, Miss Morgan really was in the most dreadful state of upset. I had certainly heard her crying, and her countenance was one of true grief. Feeling sorry for the woman, I decided to make her some hot milk and grated nutmeg and take it to her rooms in the hope that it would soothe her. She was not in her rooms when I arrived, so I determined to set the drink down and hasten to find her to let her know that it was waiting for her in her room. After I'd set the drink down, I turned to leave, and that was when I noticed her open trunk at the foot of the bed. The trunk was filled to the top with neatly folded clothing, and a quick look inside the empty wardrobe told me that everything Miss Morgan owned was, indeed, in that trunk.

At that moment I knew that she had packed to leave. The only conclusion that I could draw was that she had known of the imminent departure of her mistress and had assumed that she, too, would be going with them."

"So perhaps her grief was mixed with anger and betrayal?" Mary almost bit her tongue; the pronouncement had sounded like something from a romance novel.

"Oh, I don't doubt it." Mrs. Miller placed her teacup back onto the tray. "But I'm afraid that I really must swear you to secrecy, Miss Porter, for in truth I have never spoken of the open trunk before. I rather fear that if the Earl had found out about it, Miss Morgan would have lost her post here, and I could not have lived with that. Whatever I think of the woman herself, I should not like to see her cast adrift without warning."

"No, indeed, I agree with you entirely. And I can assure you of my complete confidence in the matter." Mary smiled reassuringly at Mrs. Miller.

"Thank you, Miss Porter. In truth, you must think it very strange of me to tell you something so confidential so very early on in our friendship. I must admit that I find I'm rather drawn to trusting you, and I am very keen to give you some background which would explain the Earl's rather sour behavior."

"Yes, indeed, how terrible for the poor man, and how he must have suffered. What a dreadful shock for anybody to cope with, particularly when a mother walks away from her own children. How very heartbreaking."

"It is heartbreaking, Miss Porter, for his Lordship has not always been so severe. It is true that he has never been an overly sociable man, and on account of it there are some who would describe him as taciturn. But I think that *that* is simply because he chooses not to engage in frivolous conversation. In the years I have worked here, I have always seen the Earl as an extremely intelligent man, and one who seemed to me to have been rather wishing for an equally intelligent wife."

"Lady Pennington was intelligent then?"

"Not in any noticeable way, I am afraid to say. Perhaps she was rather more astute than she was intelligent. It was a great surprise to me when the Earl married her, and I have to wonder if he had rather given up hope of finding a more sensible wife. That being said, he did truly seem to care for her, and her departure has caused him obvious distress."

"And presumably has caused Oliver and Isobel a great deal of distress too. For I suppose, how could it not?" Mary stared off into space sadly. "How very sad for them. The poor little children."

"I know, Miss Porter. For a child to realize that their mother has left them behind must be the most dreadful experience. In matters such as those, I'm sure there can be no difference between rich and poor. There are no compensations for that, are there?"

"No, indeed there are not. But I cannot help but think that now is the very time that they need their father's love. They need their father's involvement in their world, and not for five minutes at either end of the day in which he demands to know if they've behaved themselves."

"Again, that was not always so. In truth, I never saw a man so happy as the day those babies were born. Up until their mother left, the Earl absolutely doted on them. I simply think that the damage which Lady Pennington caused as she walked out of the door has been brutal and irreparable."

"But they need him," Mary said, not entirely disposed to completely excuse the behavior of the Earl of Pennington.

"Perhaps you should make that your mission, Miss Porter." Mrs. Miller's smile broadened. "You seem like a very sensible and intelligent woman who is more than capable of bringing the children's behavior back into something more acceptable. If you can do that then, who knows? Perhaps you will be able to help in some way to heal the rift which has rent this family apart."

"It sounds like an almost insurmountable task," Mary said, somewhat self-deprecatingly. However, the cogs of her mind were already turning, and the fact that Mrs. Miller had described it as a mission had rather encouraged Mary into thinking that she really could make a difference at Linwood Hall.

Once their tea was finished and Mary had begun to make her way back into the main part of the house, she realized that she felt very differently than she had on her way downstairs. Mrs. Miller had done much to soothe her disquiet and provide her with the background information she felt she needed to enable her to do her job properly.

However, Mary knew that it was rather more than *that* which had seen a resurgence of her old spirit. It was the fact that there was a problem here to be solved, and the very idea that she might, indeed, be just the right sort of person to solve it.

Although her very own hasty assessment of Miss Morgan had proved so negative, Mary did not think that her instincts about the woman had been entirely wrong. It was also clear that Mrs. Miller had her very own reservations about the aging nurse, and Mary was very glad to have the housekeeper's confidence in that regard.

Mary knew that the very first thing she needed to do was assess her two young charges, and find out just how deeply they had been affected by the departure of their mother. Although Mary was a most efficient teacher, she never taught or influenced by force or bullying, and had always found that kindness was a great encourager.

Above all else, Mary had a deep desire to help the children; to do whatever she could to ease the suffering of the small, angel-faced siblings.

or more than two weeks, Mary studied Oliver and Isobel extremely closely. From the very moment she had told them an extremely exciting story that very first day, just as she had promised, the children had very much taken to her. As Mary had given the two wide-eyed children a tale of pirates and shipwrecks, they had listened attentively and were visibly gripped by the amusement.

"Does your nurse tell you lots of stories?" Mary had felt compelled to ask. While she did not want to use the children as an instrument by which to find out information, she judged that to find out as much as she could about the day-to-day running of their lives could only serve to help her to reach them better.

"Miss Morgan tells us two stories out of the Bible, Miss Porter." Isobel had been the first to answer on that occasion, but she had rather given her response to her brother, as opposed to directly addressing her new governess. Seeing the little cheeks flaming pink, Mary decided to give the child time to get used to her and did not request that she look at her at all.

"But what about *other* stories? Does your nurse tell you any stories like the one I have just told you?" Mary was pushing, but she knew that she must.

"No, Miss, it is just the same two stories from the Bible all the time." This time Oliver had spoken. His confidence seemed just a little more developed than his sisters, and he shyly spoke to Mary with eyes that darted backward and forwards, almost as if they could not entirely settle upon her.

By the end of the second day, it was already clear to Mary that to begin an actual education of the children at that point would be a mistake. They were quiet, shy, and entirely unsure of themselves. They were two lost little children in a world of adults they simply did not understand.

Mary gently introduced clever and interesting games, things which would use language in a way that would allow her to determine their level of understanding. Mary had also decided upon daily exercise, most commonly nature rambles around the grounds of the estate. By the middle of the second week, the children were actively looking forward to the nature ramble every morning and had begun to talk about trees and plants and small animals. More importantly, they had begun to talk to Mary about these things, often forgetting their initial shyness.

Despite the fact that Miss Morgan now only served to get the children up and dressed in the morning, and washed and dressed ready for bed at night. Still, her reports of bad behavior continued. Initially, Mary had not realized that this was happening, since she was rarely in the company of the children again after the nurse took over in the evening.

However, the Earl had requested Mary's presence to discuss the arrangements for which she should receive her payments. With their business and the somewhat stilted accompanying conversation, almost over, Mary had still been in the drawing room when Miss Morgan had arrived with the children to say goodnight to their father.

Once again, the slight kerfuffle of the nurse telling the children to behave themselves prior to entering the room took place. Something about it made Mary frown and got her to thinking.

"Do come in, Miss Morgan," the Earl had said in an exact replica of Mary's first evening at Linwood Hall. Again, the harried-looking nurse ushered in Oliver and Isobel, both of whom studied the floor carefully as they walked through the drawing room.

"Well, children, have you been good?" the Earl said, as Mary's stomach tightened into a knot.

"Yes, Papa," Oliver and Isobel once again spoke together.

"Miss Morgan?" the Earl asked, and Mary wanted to rise to her feet and demand that the Earl and the nurse use their brains for a change.

"Well, I would not say *good* exactly, Your Lordship," Miss Morgan said, shaking her head in a most disappointed fashion.

Mary cleared her throat and twisted somewhat in her seat. Miss Morgan's eyes flew to her, clearly indicating that she had not hitherto realized that the governess was also in the room. Mary could hardly believe that the nurse could have experienced such bad behavior from Oliver and Isobel in just an hour and a half of taking charge of them. Mary had been with the children since breakfast at half past eight in the morning and had seen nothing by way of bad behavior. In truth, Mary had seen not one moment's poor behavior in the two weeks since she had been the children's governess. Something about Miss Morgan's predictable report rang rather untrue with Mary, and she could feel herself unable to stand by and do nothing.

"In what way, Miss Morgan?" Mary said, keeping her voice light and friendly, yet her eyes were pure steel as they bored into the older woman.

"I beg your pardon?" Miss Morgan returned the stare, and Mary was surprised to see exactly how determined it was. Mary could read in Miss Morgan's countenance her extreme dislike and was somewhat taken aback by the complete lack of any attempt to conceal it.

"In what way have the children misbehaved, Miss Morgan? I should very much like to know," Mary said, maintaining that lightness of voice which she truly did not feel.

"There has been a roughness of manner, and a large degree of backtalk," the nurse said after several moments contemplation. In that very moment, Mary knew that what the woman said was a lie. She had no idea why the nurse would lie about the children, she just knew that she was.

"How intriguing! I have not perceived any such behavior in the children since I have become their governess. What is that now? More than two weeks, I believe." Mary knew that her words were accusatory even though her tone was not.

The Earl seemed to sit upright in his seat, as if suddenly interested.

"Well, I daresay you should wait until you get to know them better." The nurse almost spat the words at her.

"Oh, I presume you mean that once the children are comfortable with me, they shall cease to behave themselves?" Mary looked from Miss Morgan's reddening face down to the reddening faces of Oliver and Isobel. The children seemed most uncomfortable, and Mary felt a terrible stab of guilt that she had, perhaps, been the cause of their disquiet. However, Mary realized that Isobel was rather squinting, and as she looked at Miss Morgan's big ugly hands, she could see that she was squeezing the children's little hands rather hard.

"Oh, I say!" Mary rose hurriedly to her feet and dashed across the room, dropping to her knees just in front of the children. "I rather think you're squeezing their little hands too hard, Miss Morgan."

"I beg your pardon?" The nurse's voice was beginning to rise.

"Please, let them go this minute." Mary allowed her voice to rise also. She could see tears in the eyes of both children and felt an immense wave of anger wash over her. With nothing else to do, Miss Morgan finally released her grip on the twins. Immediately, Mary took their little hands and studied them. Both were rather red, and Isobel's in particular still bore the fading print of Miss Morgan's tightly gripping fingers.

"Your Lordship!" Miss Morgan had been the first to address the Earl, in rather plaintive and disgruntled tones.

"Miss Morgan." The Earl began without moving from his seat. "Perhaps it is time you took the children off to bed now."

Mary could not believe what she was hearing. She looked up at Miss Morgan, and she could see the victory in the older woman's eyes. In truth, she wanted above all else to rise to her feet and deliver some kind of blow to the awful woman's face. Feeling her cheeks reddening and her breath quickening, Mary tried desperately to calm herself; she had never had such a violent imagining in all her life.

Still, on the floor, Mary's head snapped around as she made eye contact with the Earl. He returned her gaze with nothing more than a cold, blank stare. As she turned to face the children once more, the little hands were snatched from her by Miss Morgan, who hurriedly pulled them away from her and hastened them from the room. For some seconds, Mary found herself unable to move from her kneeling position on the floor. She was entirely stunned by the Earl's lack of intervention, and her strongest instinct was to set off after the nurse and relieve her of the two innocent children.

Finally, Mary rose to her feet and, remaining in the spot where she stood, turned to face the Earl.

"Do you mind telling me exactly what that was all about, Miss Porter?" The Earl's voice was quiet but full of authority.

"Your Lordship, I do not for one moment believe that your children are as poorly behaved as Miss Morgan continually paints them to be."

"Perhaps you and she simply have different standards, Miss Porter." His lack of concern and his seeming determination to do nothing to find out the truth of the situation was completely infuriating her.

"I have no doubt that we have vastly differing standards, Your Lordship." Mary knew that her tone was a little sarcastic. "But I can truthfully say that I have perceived no bad behavior whatsoever from your children whilst they have been in my care."

"Is this perhaps because they are currently rather overindulged in your company, Miss Porter?"

"In what way, Your Lordship?"

"I am led to believe that you spend the majority of the day in play, rather than in learning. Is that not true?"

Mary could feel her eyes squint and her brows knit together. She had seen very little of the Earl in the daytime when she had been with the children, so knew that he could not have perceived such a thing with his own eyes. So, she was being watched by somebody, and that certain somebody was reporting back to the Earl of Pennington.

"That is not true. I'm simply getting to know your children through varied activities. Some of the activities which would appear to someone else as play, are rather helpful for myself in assessing what knowledge and understanding Oliver and Isobel already have. Furthermore, they seem like rather traumatized little children to me, and I am, quite rightly, nurturing their trust in me before we head off down the path of learning to read and write and count." Mary could feel the color draining from her face under the scrutiny of his steely gaze.

"Traumatized?" That simple word, quietly spoken, had very much made Mary regret her own turn of phrase. However, she had said it, and there would be no going back.

"They are extremely quiet and shy, even for four-year-olds. They are also continually nervous, although I am pleased to say that I can see that trait easing in them whilst they are with me."

"And the source of their nervousness? In your expert opinion?" Every one of the words the Earl spoke felt like a physical slap.

"They evidently know that there is something wrong, but they are not yet equipped to deal with the emotions and the upsets of the adults around them. As a consequence of their fear and confusion mixed with constant castigation, they have very much retreated within themselves. So much so, Your Lordship, that I fail to see how such terribly introverted children could possibly be dealing in any manner of backtalk and other such similar behavior as reported by their nurse."

"Are you saying that Miss Morgan is lying?" the Earl asked, his voice had returned to the quiet and authoritative tone of earlier. At that moment, Mary rather felt like a small and frightened child herself. However, she very quickly gathered herself, and her anger fortified her.

"Yes, Your Lordship. That is exactly what I'm saying." Mary found his light blue eyes and fixed them with her own. She had determined that she would not be the first to look away.

"What possible reason can Miss Morgan have to lie about the behavior of my children?"

"I do not know what reason she could have, Your Lordship, but I do know that those children are by no means unruly. Frightened? Yes. Confused? Yes. But rude and unruly? Absolutely not."

"I'm sorry, Miss Porter, but I really can see no reason for Miss Morgan to lie to me about the behavior of my children." The Earl seemed ready to shrug the whole thing off.

"Your Lordship, just because her motives are not clear, does not mean that I am not right."

"And have my children actually *told* you they are frightened and confused?" The Earl's blank look was beginning to turn into a scowl.

"No, of course, they have not. They are but four-years-old. How on earth could you expect them to be able to explain emotions such as these? However, I do not need to hear them verbalize it, Your Lordship. I can see it!" Mary was utterly furious, and she could feel her small hands balling into fists. Quite what she expected to do with her little fists, she had no notion.

"How dare you?" The Earl shouted so suddenly that Mary almost gasped in alarm. "I do not need a woman who has been in my home but two weeks to tell me what she thinks I do and do not know about my own children." The Earl had begun to rise to his feet.

Mary stood her ground.

"And how dare you?" Mary's voice had risen enough to almost match the Earl's. "Children are a gift! Children are precious and should be treated as such. It does not matter what disappointments either you or nurse Morgan have experienced in your lives, they should not in any way impact upon tiny children who can do nothing to help you or themselves."

"I am the Earl of Pennington!"

Mary could see that he knew his comment to be ridiculous, and something about it almost made her want to laugh. However, she correctly assessed that he was asserting his authority as the employer.

"I am perfectly well aware of who you are, Your Lordship. That makes absolutely no difference whatsoever to my concerns about your children."

"I hardly think you are in a position to tell me…"

"Really? When you spend but five minutes in the morning and five minutes in the evening in their company? Can you honestly say that you know in your heart what is going on in your children's lives? Can you honestly say that you have any inkling of what they are going through and how they are feeling?" Mary was genuinely shouting, and rather wondered if any of the servants could hear her.

"Return to your room this instant and pack your things," the Earl said quietly, and turned away from her, striding towards the large window. As he stood with his back to her, Mary knew that she had been dismissed entirely. If only she could have held her temper. If only she could have explained things in a different way, perhaps he would have understood what she was trying to tell him, without taking such terrible offense. Realizing that there was now nobody to care about the hearts of those tiny children, Mary could feel tears running freely down her face. Knowing that any objection to her dismissal would be useless, Mary turned and made her way out of the drawing room.

MARY'S FURY mixed with deep turmoil had made her a rather efficient packer. Within ten minutes of being back in her large and pretty bedroom, her two trunks were all but filled with speedily, yet carefully, folded gowns. All that was left for her to do was to pack a few trinkets which she had brought from home to remind her of Denmouth and her own family.

The very thought of her wonderful father and three beautiful sisters had brought tears to her eyes. Even her father's new wife was a kind and caring woman, and Mary could see how the lives of her young sisters contrasted almost violently with those of Oliver and Isobel. As wealthy as her own family had become, it was entirely incomparable to the wealth and privilege Oliver and Isobel lived in. However, had the very walls been lined with gold, as far as Mary could see, the tiny twins might as well have had nothing in the world. For without a loving influence, or any adult in which to trust with your heart, as a child, you could get nowhere.

The very thought that her own temper had removed her from the children, depriving them of whatever love she could have shown them, increased her sobs to such an extent that she found herself almost gasping for air. After a few moments of concentrated weeping, Mary knew that she must put herself to rights. With her possessions entirely packed, Mary had absolutely no idea what move she was to make next.

The Earl had simply told her to go and pack, but had not told her if the carriage was to be ordered that very evening, or if she was simply to leave the following day. Wondering if she was, in fact, supposed to arrange her own departure in its entirety, Mary began to contemplate seeking out Mrs. Miller for assistance. Once she had decided upon that course of action, Mary sat upon the lid of one of her packing trunks in order to regain her composure in its entirety before she set off to make her way below stairs.

EMERSON RUTHERFORD STARED out of the window for some

minutes, desperately trying to regain his composure. His body had quite literally throbbed with rage, and he had studied the surrounding countryside with grim determination. As he stared, he hoped that he would quickly calm to a point where he no longer felt the need to kick furniture or sweep numerous ornaments from the oak side table.

He had hardly been able to believe what he had been hearing when Miss Mary Porter had begun to question Miss Morgan. From the moment she had begun to quiz the nurse, he had known that it was leading somewhere. There was a forthright determination about Miss Porter which would somehow not be denied. In that very moment, he had felt a certain unease creep over him, almost dreading what it was she had to say.

That she had implied a certain cruelty on behalf of the children's nurse had been hard enough for him to hear, without her brazenly following her argument up with accusations aimed at the Earl himself. As much as he knew he was right to dismiss the woman for her very conduct, still there was something inside him which made him rather wish he had simply dismissed her from the room, rather than from his home and his employment.

Even as he felt his breathing return to its normal steady pace, Emerson found himself irresistibly drawn to relive every moment of the sordid encounter. As much as he had tried to deny Miss Morgan's conduct as alleged by Miss Porter, still he could not help but apply the same reasoning to the governess. He had said that he could find no reason for Miss Morgan to lie about the conduct of his children, but by the same standard, he could find no reason for Miss Porter to lie about their *good* behavior.

Still, as the Earl of Pennington, could he really forgive her outburst? Nobody in his employment had ever, *ever* shouted at him. In truth, he could not even remember anyone in the employment of Linwood Hall ever shouting at his father when he had been the Earl. No, first and foremost, standards must be upheld.

Emerson turned from the window and made his way over to the drinks table. Pouring himself a rather large brandy, he swallowed the fiery liquid back in one gulp, before taking a deep and sudden breath to relieve the burning of his throat.

Pouring himself a second, Emerson returned to his sitting position on the couch and stared thoughtfully down into his drink. He could not help but remember how Oliver and Isobel had regarded Miss Porter when she had first begun to question their nurse's account of their behavior. He had seen something there in Oliver's little face, but what had it been? The boy had seemed to have lost his awkwardness in just that tiny moment, almost as if he was looking upon Miss Porter as his... his... *Savior? Rescuer?*

Emerson once again drained his glass in one gulp, wondering exactly why it was those words had sprung to mind. Could there have been something in what Miss Porter had said?

Of course, he *knew* there had been. There were elements of truth in what she had said which had felt like physical blows at the very time she had spoken the words.

Whilst Miss Porter had not alluded to any knowledge of the circumstances of his wife's disappearance, he had known that she must surely be very sensible of it all. The way she had spoken of the disappointments of either himself or Miss Morgan being something that the children should not be expected to suffer from had more or less confirmed it for him.

And had he really ever stopped to wonder quite how Constance's disappearance had affected their children? In truth, he had rather considered them to be too young to understand, and therefore too young to be affected by it all. They had been but three-years-old at the time, and barely even speaking coherently.

Staring somewhat determinedly down at the intricate pattern of the huge Oriental rug, Emerson began to wonder if he had, perhaps, been mistaken in his approach. Perhaps Oliver and Isobel really *had* been affected by their mother's sudden disappearance after all. And in his heart, he knew that he had withdrawn from them in the year since his wife had run away. Every day, his children, with that bright blonde hair and pale faces, grew to look more and more like Constance. Not a day went by when he was not painfully reminded, simply by their very appearance, of the wife who had left him for his Italian cousin. With a certain amount of shame, he had not previously contemplated, Emerson Rutherford knew that he had been willfully avoiding his children for more than a year. However, it was only the appearance of Miss Mary Porter which had, somewhat brutally, forced him to reflect upon what he had done. Miss Porter seemed to hint rather heavily at the children's loss, and he rather wondered if she included their father as much as their mother in that accusation.

Not one other person of his acquaintance or within his household had ever spoken to him on the issue. And yet Mary Porter, resident as governess for little more than two weeks, had sternly and volubly reproached him. Had she simply seen the truth as it was with the fresh eyes of an outsider? And had Miss Morgan, his wife's nurse in her own childhood, simply grown too old and jaded to very much care?

Emerson sighed loudly, wondering at the complete reversal of his emotions and opinions in just a matter of minutes. He had gone from anger and outrage to shame and sadness in the time it had taken him to drink down two large brandies.

CHAPTER 6

*O*nce she had decided that her nerves and countenance had calmed considerably, Mary rose from her seat on her packing trunk and made to leave her room. In the very moment that she opened the door, the Earl had risen his hand to knock. Seeing him there most unexpectedly made Mary gasp.

"Oh, I'm most terribly sorry, Miss Porter. I was about to knock."

"Indeed," Mary said, her voice returned to calm as much as his was. "I was just on my way to speak to Mrs. Miller about arranging a carriage to take me home," Mary said quite simply and without any hint of malice.

"You are packed already, Miss Porter?" The Earl asked with a vague look of surprise as he slightly craned his neck to look around her into her bedroom. Seeing both of her trunks ready for transport, he returned his gaze to Mary.

"Yes, indeed, Your Lordship, I am packed."

"And have you spoken to Mrs. Miller already?" The Earl asked, clearly searching for something.

"No, Your Lordship. I have been in my room since… since… well, I have simply been in here packing, and I have only this minute finished."

"Well, perhaps there is no need to arrange for a carriage after all," the Earl said, and Mary thought she could detect a hint of color in his face, just beneath the butterscotch tan of his skin.

"Oh, I was unsure whether or not you intended me to remain until morning, so I packed immediately in case you were asking me to leave this minute." Mary did not know what to say, and she was not entirely sure of the Earl's meaning.

"You misunderstand me, Miss Porter. I rather dismissed you in haste, and have come to tell you that there really is no need for you to leave."

"Oh," Mary said, really not knowing what she should now do or say for the best. She turned slightly and looked back over at her packed and locked trunks, unconsciously giving the impression that she would really rather go.

"I understand, of course, if you would prefer to leave. The row we had was most truly unforgivable, but I am not placing the blame of it upon you, Miss Porter," he began. "Well, not *entirely*."

"I should not have shouted, Your Lordship," Mary said in a quiet voice. In truth, Mary still held fast to the idea that she had shouted at him with every right to do so. Yet she was hastily reminded of her tortured weeping as she thought of leaving the twins behind with no adult to champion them.

Under those circumstances, Mary thought her best road would be one of capitulation.

"Indeed you should not have, Miss Porter. But then, neither should I, and as I remember it, I was the first to raise my voice." The Earl paused, seemingly to swallow. Mary could tell that he was struggling most terribly with his attempt at an apology. Once again, with the children firmly in mind, she wondered if she should do something quite against her nature, and make it somewhat easier for him.

"Your Lordship, I already care very much for your children and please believe me that I do have their best interests at heart. However, I must own that I did not handle the matter in the right way, and I should not have done or said anything to embarrass either Miss Morgan or yourself in the way that I did. Please do accept my apologies, Your Lordship."

"As you have rightly perceived, Miss Porter, my family has undergone a certain amount of upheaval in the last year. There has been a lot of pain and suffering for the three of us left behind, but I must own up to perhaps not having dealt with things quite the way that I should have. There were elements of truth in what you said to me, and I rather think that *that* in and of itself was entirely the source of my anger. After all, Miss Porter, we, none of us, like to have our shortcomings brought before us so *brutally*."

"No, indeed, Your Lordship." At that moment, Mary felt rather ashamed of her actions. Although, that very thought was enough to make her want to stamp on her own foot. She really *did not* regret a single word of what she had said to the Earl of Pennington, only she had regretted how close it had brought her to being separated from two children who, she quite rightly assessed, greatly needed her.

"But since there was some truth in what you said, I should not like to be so churlish as to see you out of a position for it," the Earl said, with the briefest of conciliatory smiles.

"Please understand, Your Lordship, that it is not the idea of being out of the position which upsets me. I genuinely have the interests of the children at my heart."

"Yes, of course," the Earl said in a manner which suggested that he would have liked to have believed her, but rather thought that someone in her position could not afford to lose a job on a point of principle.

"Because, you see, I teach children purely because of the love of the work. I have no need to work, Your Lordship, because I am independently wealthy." A part of Mary could hardly believe she had told him the truth of her circumstances, and yet she had known she had done it to fully impress upon him the truth of what she said.

"Are you?" The Earl looked suddenly stunned by her proclamation.

"Yes, I am Your Lordship. As I told you upon interview, I did indeed run a small Dame school from my father's home in Denmouth. However, some two years ago, my father became heir to the Stonewell Shipping company and has already apportioned a certain amount of his new-found wealth to myself and my three sisters. Nonetheless, Your Lordship, I found I greatly missed the satisfaction that comes from teaching a child how to read, write and reason, and that is why I so eagerly responded to your advertisement for a governess."

"Well... Goodness me." The Earl seemed genuinely lost for words. Mary could tell that he would need a certain amount of time and solitude to process what she had just told him.

"So, Your Lordship, shall I remain here as Oliver and Isobel's governess?" Mary was keen to get a definitive answer.

"Yes, perhaps that would be for the best."

"And for the time being, may I continue in my activities with the children? There really is a method there which I have tried and tested on a number of occasions, and found to work." Mary simply could not help herself. If the aging nurse was going to continue reporting back to the Earl, Mary very much wanted to know that he understood she had a firm and proper plan for the education of his children.

"Yes, but largely because I currently can find no reason to argue with you upon the subject." His sudden smile caught Mary unawares. It was fleeting, but it had been most definite and had turned his handsome face into an extremely handsome face.

Mary could think of nothing to say in response and rather wished the encounter was over so that she could unpack her things once more and put herself to bed. In truth, the whole ordeal had entirely exhausted her.

"Well, I shall say good night, Miss Porter," the Earl said, as he turned to leave.

"Good night, Your Lordship."

THE NEXT FEW weeks seemed to pass without incident. As far as she could, Mary avoided the company of Miss Morgan, who had taken to glaring at her whenever she thought she could get away with it. The children had come on in leaps and bounds and were growing more confident with each day. As much as the very thought of her dreadful argument with the Earl was something she still could almost not bear to think of, Mary had very much come to see it as a necessary evil. From the very next day, the children seemed to move closer to her. At that moment when she had dropped to her knees and removed them from the nurse's grip, they had seen an adult *finally* taking charge. In their own undeveloped and innocent way, Oliver and Isobel had come to regard her as an instrument of justice. Something they had not known they had needed but had recognized as soon as they had seen it.

From there, it had taken only two further weeks of simple activities to bring the children to the point at which Mary felt it appropriate to start their academic learning. Already they were grasping the idea of an alphabet and had very much enjoyed drawing pictures of items which represented each letter. So far, they had reached the letter G.

"So, Oliver, what shall you draw that begins with the letter G?" Mary had asked, a bright and encouraging smile on her face. For a few moments, Oliver squinted in concentration, desperately trying to think of something which began with the letter G.

"Try to think of the G as a *guh.* Then try to think of words or things which start with *guh,* Oliver."

"G…g…g… gate!" Oliver's triumph culminated in an excited shout. Mary could not help but laugh at his excited little face. As Mary laughed quite openly, she was rather surprised to hear little Isobel laughing also.

"I'm going to draw a goat, Miss Porter!" Isobel was so excited she almost shouted too.

"That sounds like a lovely idea, Isobel." Mary was still laughing. She was gratified to see that, without any prompting at all, Oliver and Isobel happily set about drawing the gate and the goat. Mary could not help but think that it often took very much longer to get a child to the point at which they were keen and excited to learn. Perhaps with Oliver and Isobel, her determination to do what was right for them had driven her on to greater results.

Mary looked at the two little children, side-by-side in the cozy little schoolroom. They were both bent so far over and intent on their work that their little noses were just about on the paper, and she almost laughed out loud to see that both children were slightly sticking their tongues out in concentration. They really were so very alike, and so very sweet, that Mary could feel her heart swell with feeling for them. Happy that they were both entirely engaged in their work, Mary silently sauntered over to the large window and stared out over the lush green lawns.

The views across the Linwood Hall estate were truly beautiful, as were those across the open countryside which surrounded them on all sides. Mary looked out to the east where the rolling hills rose up just a little higher than everywhere else. She smiled at the thought of her hometown of Denmouth being just out of view on the other side of those beautiful green hills. Imagining her father and Ann in the little drawing room, sharing a pot of tea and laughing over some silly conversation, Mary felt a little tug to her heart.

Smiling to herself, Mary turned her gaze in the other direction, seeking out the small plot of earth which Perkins, the gardener, had allowed her and the children to use for growing their own flowers. Mary had enjoyed the pastime almost as much as Oliver and Isobel and had given them free rein with what grew where. As a consequence, the little patch was becoming a riot of mismatched colors and disproportionate heights. Still, the children had been extremely proud of their achievements, as was Mary.

As Mary craned her neck to get a good view of the little plot, her eyes widened to see the Earl standing over it, looking down at the myriad of blooms. He was, as ever, entirely alone as he gazed down, hands listlessly thrust into his pockets, standing sideways on to Mary's point of view. Mary strained her eyes in a bid to get an idea of his expression, and yet she could make out nothing. The Earl was simply too far away from her.

In truth, the plot was so tiny, that there really was not a great deal to see, and yet the Earl maintained his position for some minutes. Just when Mary thought he was rooted to the spot, the Earl moved to the other side of the little plot and crouched down as if to get a closer look. After a few more minutes, Mary thought she could see his shoulders shake just a little, and smiled to herself when she realized that the Earl was laughing. Picturing the haphazard little blooms, Mary could quite understand his mirth, and quietly chuckled to herself.

"Miss Porter, are you laughing?" Isobel's tiny and enquiring voice brought Mary back into the room.

"Yes, Isobel, I was laughing a little."

"What were you laughing at, Miss Porter?" Oliver joined the conversation without looking up from his artwork.

"Oh, I was just thinking about my little sisters and some of the silly games they used to play." Mary could not think why she had told the white lie, except that she did not really know how to explain their father's presence at the little garden patch. After all, he still did not spend any more time with them than he had been doing when Mary arrived at Linwood Hall.

When Oliver and Isobel seemed, once more, to be entirely consumed by their own efforts, Mary turned her gaze back to the little garden plot. The Earl was rising to his feet and, as he turned to make his way back towards the house, he hurriedly wiped across both eyes with the back of his hand. Mary's mouth fell open just a little in surprise at the movement. Perhaps he was wiping away tears of mirth, and yet Mary had a heavy feeling in the very pit of her stomach. Something about his posture as he slowly walked away made Mary realize that he had not been laughing at all, but rather he had been crying. He strode somewhat purposefully across the lawns, and very quickly went out of sight. With one hand over her mouth, Mary stared resolutely out across the countryside, blinking hard at the sudden tears which had welled in her own eyes.

"It might not be exactly as I think it was, Mrs. Miller, I could be wrong. After all, if one has tears of mirth, they must still be wiped away in the same fashion, must they not?" For some days after Mary had seen the Earl by the little garden plot, she still could not shake the image of him from her mind. Finally, she gave in and raised it as a topic for discussion at one of her ever more frequent early morning visits to the housekeeper. At first, Mary had rather wondered if Mrs. Miller was so busy in the early hours that she was rather hampering the woman by continually seeking her out. However, after she had missed a couple of mornings, Mrs. Miller had sought her out to ensure that everything was alright, and had expressed a wish that Mary would resume their early morning tea and gossip.

Mary had very much given up on her previous standard of a life without gossip and had found herself being more open with Mrs. Miller than she had with any other friend before.

"I think you must follow your instinct on that question, Miss Porter; after all, it was his very *bearing* which led you to the conclusion that they were not happy tears."

"And you think I should trust my instincts?"

"Always!" Both women laughed as Mrs. Miller reached for the teapot once more.

"Is something else troubling you, Miss Porter?" Mrs. Miller continued.

"Well, yes, I rather think there is something." Mary chewed thoughtfully at her bottom lip as she stared into her teacup. "You see, after that dreadful row that I had with the Earl, I rather thought he'd understood what I'd said about the children being so very lost."

"Yes, from what you said of his responses, it would certainly seem that way."

"And yet he sees no more of them. Oh, I don't know! I just thought that once he had begun to admit things to himself, things might be a little different. I thought he might start taking more of an interest in the children."

"Perhaps he thinks it is not quite as simple as that? Perhaps he thinks that the children will never forgive him for his distance."

"Oh, how I wish I could explain to him that children do not

see the world in the same way as adults. They do not bear grudges, and they are open to love without any barriers."

"Well, I daresay after the last time you had a conversation with the Earl, you might very well need to tread carefully, and perhaps be a little more tactful." Mrs. Miller's eyes twinkled with amusement, and Mary laughed and slowly shook her head.

"Oh, Mrs. Miller!" Mary was still laughing, her cheeks reddening. "I still cannot think of it without cringing."

"Oh, my dear girl, I am just teasing you! Think of all the good that came of it. Think of how much the children have warmed to you, and how you've been able to affect their lives for the better."

"Thank you, Mrs. Miller. You really are so very kind, and I do not know what I should do without you."

"Now listen, if this business with the Earl and his children is bothering you to this extent, then I think you really must speak to him. But this time, just plan what you are going to say before you say it, and do what you can to keep the fiery side of your nature in check."

"Mrs. Miller, I do believe that you are right. I really must speak to him."

OVER THE NEXT couple of days, Mary had rather hoped for an opportunity to speak with the Earl. She had, as Mrs. Miller had advised, already prepared what it was that she wanted to say. The Earl, however, seemed to be more elusive than ever. Mary continually hovered by the schoolroom door, ever hopeful that she might catch him striding past.

Unfortunately for Mary, on the one occasion she *had* seen him, the Earl had simply ignored her completely, his countenance quite thunderous, as he strode past and made his way to his study. Once he had gained it, he firmly slammed the door behind him.

Mary had determined to be rather more sensible about things than she had the first time she had spoken to him. If Lord Pennington was in some dreadful sort of mood, then Mary rightly gathered that this was certainly not the time to suggest that he was still not spending enough time with his children.

However, day after day, the Earl seemed to shut himself away in his study and remain there for hour upon hour. Mary rather sensed that there was something wrong, and could do nothing to force herself to approach that study door and gently knock upon it. As the days passed, Mary began to despair of ever getting the opportunity to converse with the Earl.

In the end, Mary determined that, if the Earl remained cloistered within his study, that she would, indeed, approach him. After all, she had absolutely no idea how long his sour mood would continue, and rather thought that the matter could not wait forever. Unfortunately, with her decision made, Mary herself had begun to feel unwell. She had developed a most dreadful and rattling cough, which seized her periodically. The intensity of the coughing had finally made her ache and feel somewhat bruised, and she could not even clear her throat without hugging her own chest tightly first as if to brace it.

By the third day of her illness, the infection truly had her in its grasp, rendering her one moment frozen, and another almost too hot to breathe. Her arms and legs ached dreadfully, and she could barely find enough energy to set the children the simple task of drawing whatever they wished, all day long.

"Are you still feeling so unwell, Miss Porter?" Isobel's concerned face was enough to melt the hardest of hearts.

"I'm rather afraid I am, Isobel," Mary said, pulling her thick woolen shawl tightly about her, suddenly feeling very cold. "And I'm so sorry that you are left to draw all day long again whilst I keep to my chair."

"Perhaps you should go to bed, Miss Porter," Oliver added, helpfully.

"Oh, I shall be all right, but thank you, Oliver, you are very kind." Mary's gaunt and ashen face broke into a warm smile. She could not admit to the children that the only reason she had even been able to get out of bed was the very idea that they would be left for an entire day with Miss Morgan. In their childish innocence and haste to do and say whatever would please their governess, the children themselves had not considered the issue of who would take over their care from Miss Porter.

"Miss Porter, if we are to carry on with our drawings, we shall very soon need some more paper," Isobel spoke quietly, almost as if to soothe her beloved governess.

"Well, you carry on with what you have for now, and shortly I shall go and speak to your Papa and ask him for some more paper."

"Thank you, Miss Porter," Isobel said, as she looked out over her small and neat desk.

As Mary watched the children happily concentrating on their drawings, she felt somewhat mesmerized by it all. She could feel her eyelids beginning to close but seemed somehow powerless to keep herself awake. Maybe just a few moments with her eyes shut would somehow make her feel a little better.

EVERY TIME EMERSON read the letter, it felt as dreadful and shocking as the first time. For several days he had shut himself away in his study, simply looking at the communication and staring off into space wondering what on earth he should do about it. The more he sat, and the more he read, the more alone he felt.

There was no one to help him, nor anybody in whom he could confide. After all, the contents of the letter had rather made seeking another person's confidence entirely impossible. For, in truth, who could keep such shocking information to themselves?

Emerson picked up the letter once again, and almost blindly began to read. By now he knew every word and every mark of punctuation by heart, and yet he could not take his eyes from the page. How could Constance have been so very cruel? Had she not punished him enough by making a fool of him and running away with his cousin? Now why on earth would she need such vast sums of money? After all, Count Costanzo was an extremely wealthy man.

Of course, he knew he had enough money to pay her off with relative ease, and yet something held him back. In his heart, he knew that it would not end there. If he paid, Constance would come back for more, and there would never, *ever* be any real confidence that she would say nothing more on the matter.

Emerson turned the paper over in his hand, and once again he read the last few sentences on the back. The page was becoming worn, the paper softening with every handling of it.

"PLEASE BELIEVE me when I tell you I shall not think twice about exposing the whole thing, and revealing to all everything that I know."

AS EMERSON READ, he could clearly and accurately hear his wife's voice speaking the very words. At that moment, all ideas of love for her were gone. The only good thing to have come from this dreadful communication was his sudden release from the sadness caused by her departure. They had never truly been a good match, and yet he had found that he loved her. Maybe it was duty that made that love, but she was his wife, and they had children together. In his eyes living that close one had to have love. Yet, in the time it had taken to read two sides of paper, every vestige of that love had been destroyed, and Lord Pennington was finally free of it. However, as is often the case, the departure of one problem heralds the arrival of a fresh one.

If the contents of the letter in his hand ever became known, its painful effects would not simply last a year or two; they would last forever. They would ruin his life and the lives of his children.

In truth, Emerson had always assumed that Constance must have struggled dreadfully with the idea of leaving her children behind, and perhaps never seeing them again. He had never been able to believe that she had simply been able to switch off her feelings for Oliver and Isobel as she strode off in the direction of a new life without them.

Laying the letter down on the desk and leaning back in his chair once more, Emerson finally realized that he had only been fooling himself. If Constance went through with her threat, her very own children would live out the rest of their lives in poverty and shame. Not only was Constance aware of that, but she had rather alluded to it in her letter, presumably to further push Emerson to accede to her demand.

Emerson had thought and thought and could come to no conclusion. Knowing that he had been in his study for far too many days, he decided that the fresh air of the estate grounds might very well help him to look at the whole sordid mess with fresh eyes. Finally reaching his decision, Emerson rose from his desk and strode purposefully out of the room.

CHAPTER 7

$\mathcal{M}$ary woke with a start and, having no idea how long she had been asleep, quickly rose to her feet to see what the children were doing. As she stood, her thick woolen shawl fell to the floor, and she bent down to retrieve it. At that moment she felt so terribly dizzy and weak that she almost fell to the floor herself. However, she managed to pull herself upright again, using the chair for stability.

"I'm terribly sorry, children, but I fell asleep," Mary said, slowly wrapping the shawl about her shoulders once more. Her head was beginning to throb horribly, and far from feeling better for a few moments sleep, Mary felt decidedly worse.

Mary knew that she really ought to be in bed and that she probably could not continue her day feeling as ill as she did. The very thought that the children would be left with their nurse made her feel even worse, and yet she knew that she must do something.

Determining that she should go to the Earl's study and speak to him about it, Mary cast her eyes at Oliver and Isobel as she went. From somewhere they had somehow managed to get some more paper and, somewhat confusedly, Mary wondered where they might have found some. As she squinted her eyes in curiosity to see what they were drawing, Mary gasped. Some of the paper that the children were drawing on had handwriting upon it, and Mary very quickly realized that it must be correspondence.

"Oliver, Isobel? Where did you get that paper from?" Through the pain of her throbbing head, Mary felt the most dreadful of misgivings.

"From Papa's study," Isobel supplied, helpfully.

"Oh, I see. Did you go to see your Papa whilst I was asleep?" The longer Mary was on her feet, the worse she felt.

"We went to his study, Miss Porter, but Papa wasn't there."

"So he didn't give you the paper that you are drawing on?" Mary's heart had begun to thump.

"No, Miss Porter, but it was on Papa's desk, so we just took a few sheets," Oliver said, reaching to the small pile of paper as if to take another piece. As he did so, Mary gently took the paper from him, quickly realizing that it was a letter.

"Oh, children. Now I must ask you to stop drawing on the paper for the moment, if you will," Mary said in as calm a tone as possible. After all, they were only four-years-old, and they had taken the paper in innocence. She did not want them made upset about it all.

Mary could feel beads of cold sweat breaking out over her entire body and reached up to pat at her damp forehead with the corner of her shawl. As she did so, she looked briefly at the paper in her hand, to see if there were any markings upon it. She was relieved to note that the children had not drawn on that particular piece, but was suddenly struck by something on it which had caught her eye.

"I know that you are not the Earl of Pennington, and very soon everybody else will know it too."

"What?" Mary said quietly to herself.

Suddenly there was a clattering of footsteps outside in the corridor. Feeling suddenly terribly lightheaded, Mary could only look up as the door of the little schoolroom flew open and a furious Lord Pennington strode in towards her.

"What is all this? Why are my papers in here?"

"Your Lordship, forgive me," Mary said, fighting to stay conscious. "I'm afraid I fell asleep in my chair, and the children took some paper from your study to draw upon." Mary began to sway a little, and the Earl looked at her somewhat quizzically. Suddenly, his eyes flew down to the paper in her hand and, seeming to recognize it, he once again fixed his gaze upon her face.

"It is my fault, Your Lordship, not the children's. You see, I knew they were running out of paper, and I had told them that I would go to you for some more. Seeing that I was asleep, they very likely just... just......" Mary blinked hard and continuously, trying to wipe away the blackness which seemed to be forming in front of her eyes. Seeing that she was clearly unwell, the Earl seemed to forget his rage momentarily and actually began to reach for her.

"Miss Porter, are you quite well?" he asked, somewhat redundantly.

The heat which was swirling around her head and neck felt

horribly like hot needles, and Mary could hear her own breathing become labored. Finally, unable to fight it any longer, Mary's vision faded entirely as she fell sideways in a dead faint.

MARY WAS aware that she was laying down in bed, and was sensible enough to realize that it was most likely her own bed at Linwood Hall. Once or twice her eyelids had fluttered in an attempt to see who it was who was in the room with her. As unwell as she felt, Mary was convinced that she could perceive a person sitting by her bed, and was determined that she would discover who it was.

With the most dreadfully blurred vision, Mary rather thought that the person sitting at the side of her bed was, in fact, Lord Pennington. Blinking hard to clear her vision, she tried in vain to focus upon the figure. As she did so, her head began to throb horribly once more, and the pain of it made her feel nauseous. In the end, Mary decided that it must surely be Mrs. Miller sitting in the chair and that her illness had led her to hallucinate, or something similar, and her mind had tricked her that the Earl himself was sitting in her bedroom. If she'd have had the strength, Mary would have laughed at her ridiculous assumption. Instead, she simply slid back into unconsciousness, all the better to hide from her headache.

DESPITE BEING in and out of consciousness, Mary felt sure that she had sensed a certain passing of time. Now and again she had heard the sound of low voices as if two people were talking in hushed tones in her very bedroom. No doubt the doctor had been called for, and more than likely the voice was his, giving instruction to Mrs. Miller, or one of the maids, and how best to look after their patient.

"Are you quite sure, My Lord?" Mary began to rouse and felt certain that she was listening to the voice of her dear friend, Mrs. Miller.

"Absolutely, Mrs. Miller. It's time you took some rest yourself, especially since we cannot be sure that Mary's infection is not contagious." At the sound of the Earl's voice, Mary's eyes almost opened. But surely she was still far from lucid, for she could have sworn that Lord Pennington had used her Christian name.

"I could send up one of the maids, My Lord?" Once again, Mary was sure she could hear Mrs. Miller.

"Please do not trouble yourself, Mrs. Miller. After all, you have already lost one of your maids to the care of my children for the time being, and I should not deprive you further. Really, if Miss Porter wakes, I shall come and find you. I am simply sitting here as a watchman, and nothing else."

"You are very kind, Your Lordship. I'm sure that Miss Porter, once she's recovered, shall be most terribly grateful to you."

"Now do take some rest, Mrs. Miller, or that shall be *both* of my best employees laid up with sickness." The Earl laughed lightly, almost self-consciously.

"Well, I shall heed you, My Lord, and be on my way."

"Thank you, Mrs. Miller."

Hearing the door creak gently open and then close again, Mary rather guessed that Mrs. Miller had quit the room.

Although her eyes were still closed, Mary felt herself to be almost entirely conscious, notwithstanding her throbbing head and aching limbs. As the conversation had continued, Mary felt sure that she was, in fact, lucid, and that the Earl indeed had remained in the room and was, at that moment, sitting in the chair just a few feet from her bed.

Mary decided to keep her eyes closed a few moments longer while she did what she could to order her thoughts. Surely she had fainted in the schoolroom, that much was clear. As she racked her brains for information, Mary could remember that the Earl himself had been in the room at the very moment she had lost consciousness. But there was something else, surely? Some crisis or other?

As Mary tried to recollect what she suspected was a most traumatic event, her head began to throb in earnest. Unable to lay still anymore, she shifted on the bed and reached up with both hands, which she clamped tightly on either side of her forehead. Squeezing her temples rather firmly provided a certain amount of pain relief, and she sighed loudly as a result.

"Miss Porter?" Came the Earl's voice, full of concern.

"I shall be fine, Your Lordship. It's simply that my head throbs so, and seemingly only squeezing it shall provide me yet with any relief." Mary could hardly recognize her own voice. It sounded weak and reedy, and full of pain and exhaustion.

"The doctor has left us some morphine powders for you, and has given instructions on their dose." Mary could hear the Earl rise to his feet and make his way across the room to the side table. Presumably, the doctor had left her some medications on that table, and the Earl was, at that moment, mixing things just as prescribed.

"Yes, please. Thank you. Yes, please," Mary said, somewhat desperately. As hard as she was squeezing her temples, the headache was doing what it could to fight for victory over her.

"I shall be just a moment. The doctor suspects that the chest infection which, Mrs. Miller informed him, you've had for some *days*, has rather spread throughout your body. He has left an assortment of medicines, which I shall make up for you presently. But I think that perhaps the pain relief should come first."

"Yes, please," Mary said, as she moved her palms over her eyes and, quite literally, pressed down hard upon them.

Suddenly, the Earl was at her side and, placing an arm around her shoulders to gently raise her to a near sitting position, he put the cool glass against her lips.

"Now drink this, Miss Porter." He tilted the glass and Mary began to swallow down the cold, bitter-tasting fluid. It tasted so vile that she almost struggled to get away. "No, Miss Porter, you really must drink it all. Please."

Mary made a fresh attempt to finish the foul medicine, leaning heavily upon the Earl's supporting arm. The drink had made her feel suddenly cold again, and she could clearly perceive the warmth of his skin through the sleeve of his shirt. The sudden intensity made her shudder a little, and Lord Pennington gently laid her back down upon her pillows.

Mary's hands resumed their position on her eye sockets, and she lay in silence in that fashion for some fifteen minutes.

"Oh, I say!" she began. "I feel most unusually giddy."

"That will be the morphine, it rather makes one feel that one is floating," the Earl said, gently. "And how is the pain, Miss Porter?"

"Oh, I rather think it is going," Mary said, almost as if she was not entirely sure. Gently, she released the pressure she had been putting on her eyes with her palms, and she experimentally opened and closed her eyes for a few seconds. "Oh, yes, that is very much better."

"Thank goodness." The Earl said as he lifted his chair with ease and drew it closer to the bed.

Now that she was thinking somewhat more clearly, Mary really did begin to wonder why it was that her employer had chosen to sit by her bedside and see her through her illness.

"I am most terribly grateful for your kindness, Your Lordship, but I am rather wondering why you *yourself* have chosen to tend to me." Mary was relieved to hear that there was not a single note of ingratitude in her tone.

"Well, I rather wanted to speak to you, Miss Porter, as soon as you woke up. You see, I feel most dreadfully guilty about you fainting like that. Whatever the reasons, I should never, ever have shouted at you so loudly."

Mary blinked again and stared at the ceiling; those last few moments before she fell unconscious were slowly dripping back into her confused and tired mind. When all of the details were once again fresh, Mary groaned a little at the thought of the children drawing on their father's important paperwork.

"I really am most terribly sorry, Miss Porter." The Earl continued his apology with the utmost sincerity.

"Oh, I did not faint because you shouted at me, Your Lordship! I was simply unwell." Mary shifted her gaze to look at her employer.

"Oh, I could see that, Miss Porter. You looked absolutely appalling," the Earl said, his countenance most earnest.

"Oh." Mary almost laughed at his unintentional insult.

"Oh, I say! Once again, I am most dreadfully sorry. That was not a terribly flattering thing to say, was it?"

"In truth, Your Lordship, it was not the most flattering thing I've ever heard. But I shall not hold it against you." Mary was surprised to hear herself laugh a little. She was equally surprised to find that the laughter did not hurt her in any way. "I had really been feeling rather unwell for days, Your Lordship, and I should really have said something and taken a day or two in bed to recover from it before I got to this state."

"And I shouldn't have minded, Miss Porter. I realize that we have not been on the best terms, but I should never have expected you to continue to work whilst you were so unwell."

"You misunderstand, My Lord. I did not think that you would force me to work through illness, I was just worried that the children would be left all day with…." Mary stopped herself just in time. However, it would have been clear to anybody that she was about to finish her sentence with *Miss Morgan*. And while she was feeling most dreadfully unwell, Mary knew that she would not be equal to any argument that would undoubtedly be caused by airing her views about the aging nurse again.

"With Miss Morgan?" the Earl said, seemingly unaffected by

it. "No, Oliver and Isobel are in the care of one of the housemaids. I asked Mrs. Miller to see to it, and she has placed the children in the care of Daisy for the last couple of days."

"Really?" Mary felt such a sudden wave of relief wash over her that it almost surprised her. She knew that she cared greatly for the twins, but until that moment had no idea quite how much. As sick as she was, she simply could not have borne the thought of the children being left at the mercy of their nurse. Closing her eyes for a few brief moments, she gave up a silent prayer of thanks that they had not been forced to suffer such an ordeal. Their confidence and spirit had grown so much in the weeks since Mary had been their governess, that she could not bear to see them slide back again into uncertainty, fear, and near-silence.

"Although I suspect that any idea of teaching will have gone out of the window, Miss Porter. When I last checked upon them, they were fully engaged in helping Daisy rub wax polish into a small side table in the drawing room." Lord Pennington shrugged in a way which made Mary laugh. He studied her for just a few moments before allowing himself to laugh also. "I have to say, they looked as if they were really rather enjoying themselves."

"I'm sure they were, Your Lordship. They are extremely good little children, and they absolutely throw themselves into every activity, no matter what it is." Mary's relief that the children were with Daisy was making her somewhat gregarious. "They even have a little plot in the garden; you really should see them digging and planting. They seem to like to get their hands dirty."

"Oh, yes, I've seen all of their flowers. What a very nice idea. How clever of you to come up with such a thing."

Mary could have bitten through her own tongue as the recollection of the day she had seen him crouching by the flower bed came rushing back to her. Wanting to change direction entirely, Mary decided to find out more about Miss Morgan.

"But Miss Morgan still gets the children up in the morning and takes care of them in the evening, Your Lordship?"

"Well, no. Daisy has taken full care of them since you became ill. I rather thought that they might suffer somewhat in your absence and that perhaps it would be best to keep them with young Daisy in the interim."

"And Miss Morgan?" Mary could do nothing to hide her curiosity.

"I simply told her that, since the children spent much of their time with you, they might very well be carrying some infection. She seemed more than pleased to relinquish control of them, at any rate."

"You believe me, don't you?" Mary said, her voice so quiet it was almost inaudible.

"I do *now*, Miss Porter. Having seen how very different the children are with you, I finally understood why you were so suspicious of Miss Morgan's bad reports of them. I still do not understand *why*, but I have thought about it for long enough to realize that it's true."

"But what shall you do with her? I mean, once I am well, won't Miss Morgan expect to have charge of the children in the morning and evening again?"

"Well, I have bought some time in which to think about how to proceed, and believe me, I shall be giving it a great deal of thought, Miss Porter."

"Oh, yes, of course, please do forgive my intrusion. I think the morphine is making me rather talkative."

"Please, do not make yourself uneasy about that." The Earl began to laugh again, and Mary could not help but notice how handsome it made his face. His laughter, although brief, seemed to reach all the way up into his eyes, making them twinkle.

"Miss Porter, I am afraid there is something else about which I must speak with you." The Earl's very sudden change of countenance almost made Mary sit up in her bed.

"Indeed, Your Lordship?" Mary could hear the worry in her own voice but truthfully could not begin to imagine what the Earl could possibly have to say to her, especially with such a look of seriousness upon his face.

"Yes, it's rather awkward, if I'm completely honest."

"Oh, dear."

"You see, just before you fell ill, the children were using some of my papers for drawing on."

"Yes, Your Lordship, I remember. But it really wasn't their fault."

"No, indeed. And it was not your fault either, Miss Porter. It was simply unfortunate." Mary was somewhat relieved to see a brief but reassuring smile play upon his lips. "But there was a piece of correspondence in amongst that paperwork, the piece you held in your hand, in fact." The Earl paused and looked at her, seemingly searching for a clue of some sort.

"I know that you are not the Earl of Pennington, and very soon everybody else will know it too." The line which Mary had inadvertently read came rushing back to her, and her mouth

dropped open a little before she had thought to hide her knowledge of the subject.

"I perceive, Miss Porter, that you have an idea of the contents of that letter." Although the Earl's voice was low, Mary could not hear anything accusatory in it.

"I did not intentionally read the letter, Your Lordship. I simply saw something on it whilst I was checking it over for any marks from the children," Mary said, completely truthfully.

"From the look on your face, Miss Porter, I can see that what you saw was likely to be the most pertinent part of that correspondence."

"I'm rather afraid that you might be right, Your Lordship. I really am most terribly sorry about it."

"It is not your fault, Miss Porter. Please do not think that I blame you for it, despite the way I acted at the time."

"Really, Your Lordship...." Mary had begun before the Earl spoke again.

"I realize that you and I did not get off to the best start, and I have no doubt that you have many reasons to despise me. I must tell you that, if ever you thought of a revenge upon me, that letter is undoubtedly the way with which to take it."

"Why on earth should I seek to take revenge upon you?" Mary could hear a certain strident tone in her voice and realized that she had not deployed that since she was teaching a rather unruly child in her Dame school. In truth, she was momentarily gratified to see the Earl look utterly chastised by her. "Oh, I'm terribly sorry, Your Lordship. I was just rather surprised at the idea that you think I should seek some revenge upon you. I mean, I really can see no reason for it. And as for my despising you... well, I simply do not. I have no reason to."

"Thank you, Miss Porter. I cannot tell you how gratified I am to hear you say such a thing."

"It is the truth, Your Lordship. Believe me when I tell you that you have *nothing* to fear from me. Believe me when I tell you that my confidence in the matter is *entirely* inviolate."

"I am so greatly relieved, Miss Porter. For you see, if the assertion is true and goes on to become public knowledge, then everything I have shall be forfeit. In truth, my children and I should no longer be able to remain here, nor access any of the funds of the estate."

Mary's mind was absolutely reeling. She had only seen that one terrible sentence in the entire correspondence but had not assumed for one moment that it could possibly be true.

"*If* the assertion is true?" Mary said, her voice full of confusion.

"Yes, Miss Porter. It may be true, and it may not be. In truth, I do not know one way or the other. I have been wandering around with the knowledge of it weighing heavily upon my shoulders for the last few days, and still, I can settle upon no course of action."

Mary could perceive something in his countenance which seemed almost like relief to her. Perhaps she was the only person with whom he had discussed it, albeit in such a small way.

"I do not wish to pry, Your Lordship, but I am rather afraid that I do not understand," Mary said.

"Perhaps it would be easier, Miss Porter, if I made you

sensible of the entire contents of the letter," the Earl said, quietly.

"Of course, you may tell me, Your Lordship, but please know that I do not *demand* it." Mary attempted to raise herself up to a sitting position. She was beginning to find it most disconcerting to attempt to have such a conversation with Lord Pennington while she was laying completely flat. Mary rather felt that she needed to be sitting up and looking at him most squarely before he told her anything further.

Realizing what she was trying to do, the Earl hurriedly rose from his seat and gently helped her to sit up. With his arm about her shoulders once more, he almost pulled her to him as he reached around with his other arm and arranged the pillows more appropriately for sitting. As he worked, Mary found her face almost nuzzled into the side of his neck, and as she breathed in, she could sense the warmth of his skin and smell the clean scent of him. It truly seemed most intimate, and yet at the same time, not at all offensive to her. In truth, this sort of attention should really have been paid to her by one of the female staff members, and yet at that moment, she was rather glad that it was not so.

Once he had arranged the pillows, Lord Pennington gently helped her to lean back against them.

"Is that a little more comfortable, Miss Porter?" he asked, so matter-of-factly that Mary could have laughed. Either he was so distressed by his letter that he had forgotten some of the social proprieties, or he was little bothered with them in the first place. In truth, Mary could not figure out which.

"Yes, very much more comfortable, I thank you," Mary said, feeling a little flustered but determined not to show it. "Do continue, Your Lordship."

"Oh, yes, of course. As I was saying, it is probably going to be easier if I simply tell you the whole thing."

"Then let me assure you, Your Lordship, that whatever you tell me is now, and forever shall remain, in complete confidence."

"And I thank you for it, Miss Porter." The Earl stopped for a moment and drew in rather a large breath. "Well, to begin at the beginning, a few days ago I received a letter with an Italian postmark. I immediately realized that it must surely be a correspondence from my wife, Lady Constance Pennington. You see, well I'm sure you are aware, that my wife rather took off for Italy with a distant cousin of mine around a year ago." He looked at Mary for confirmation.

"Yes, Your Lordship. I was rather aware of it," Mary said simply. At that moment she had realized that there would be little point in feigning ignorance of the subject. He was about to bare his soul to her, and she knew she would be serving him very ill to patronize him in any way.

"So you see, I was somewhat taken aback before I had even opened the thing. After all, I have heard nothing whatsoever from her since she left. In fact, I could really only ever *surmise* that she had run away with Count Costanzo... they both simply vanished at the same time, you see? Anyway, I think I knew it in my heart, and the Italian postmark upon the envelope was simply a confirmation of everything I had hitherto suspected."

"Oh, dear, I am most terribly sorry, Your Lordship," Mary said, her voice low and respectful.

"I must say, I rather wish the shocks had ended there. When I opened the letter and read it through, I could scarcely believe the contents. I can honestly tell you, Miss Porter, that I have never felt such shock in all of my life."

Mary could think of nothing to say to fill the gap he had left with his moment of silence. Instead, she simply nodded at him, encouraging him to continue with his story.

"I had fully expected it to be some sort of dreadful explanation as to her actions, or even a simple confirmation that she had, indeed, left for Italy. However, there was nothing of the sort. There was not even any mention of our children, nor any inquiry as to their health and well-being." Lord Pennington stopped for a moment and shook his head bitterly. "It was simply a letter of blackmail, pure and simple."

"Blackmail?" Mary knew that her eyes were as wide as saucers, yet could do nothing to temper her expression.

"Yes, Miss Porter, blackmail. You see, my wife claims to have been told some years ago that I am not, indeed, my father's true son. She claims, therefore, that I have no right to the title of Earl, and that if I do not accede to her requests, then she shall search for the proper proof of it all, and make it known. Once she has done that, I shall have no claim to Linwood Hall nor any of my fortune. As she rightly points out, the title and the inheritance shall *all* fall upon my next of kin. In my case, a distant cousin."

"Oh, dear God!" Mary said, somewhat more indelicately than she had intended to. "Not the Italian Count, surely?" To admit to knowing that Count Costanzo was, indeed, the Earl's cousin, was to admit that she had been furnished with the complete details of the scandal. However, at that moment, Mary could not see how it mattered anymore.

"Oh, no, no. My next of kin is a distant cousin on my father's side, living somewhere in Shropshire. In truth, I have not seen him in years. We are not close and, like most men, he would not hesitate to seize control of my title and my estate, I am sure of it."

"Then your wife's intention in the matter was not to secure your fortune in its entirety? Then I don't understand, what can she possibly get from it all?"

"She has sent me a very specific request."

At that moment, Mary felt an almost physical pain in her chest. Surely Lady Pennington had not demanded he send their children over to Italy. She could have cried in that instant. The poor twins had been through enough to last them a lifetime.

"Not the children!" Mary heard the tremor in her voice and could do nothing to hide the emotion.

"Oh, no, not the children." The Earl shook his head and reached out as if to pat her. Rather thinking better of it at the last moment, he simply patted the edge of the bed itself. "No indeed, she did not mention the children once. Instead, she has asked me for an amount of money."

"As despicable as that is, Your Lordship, would it not simply be safer to just pay her?" Mary said, rather wondering if the amount which had been requested was simply too crippling to contemplate.

"In truth, at this stage, it probably would be. However, I cannot help but think that, should she find her proof, it would not end there. It would not be one simple payment, and as you rightly showed concern for the children before, I cannot rule out that she might one day demand I send them to her."

"Yes, of course. But really, what proof could she possibly

have? If it is nothing more than idle gossip, or some tawdry allegation of an affair on your mother's part, surely there is no real way of proving it?" Mary could not believe that she was sitting up in bed discussing the fact that the Earl's late mother might have had an illicit love affair whilst married to his father.

The Earl was silent for a few moments before continuing.

"It's nothing quite as simple as that, I'm afraid. The entire story is rather more credible than you might think."

At that very moment, there came a light tapping at the door. Mary and the Earl fixed one another with a startled gaze, almost as if they had been caught doing something they should not be doing.

"It will no doubt be Mrs. Miller, come to see how you are." The Earl began to rise and make his way to the door. "With your permission, I shall return later," the Earl said the last in an almost inaudible whisper. Mary simply nodded her consent to his request as he reached for the door handle.

"Ah, Mrs. Miller. I hope you are rested. I am pleased to report that our patient is finally awake."

CHAPTER 8

"*Well*, I can honestly say, Miss Porter, that I have never seen the Earl take to the bedside of a sick member of staff before now! He enquires, obviously, but this!" Mrs. Miller's eyes were open wide as she spoke to Mary, clearly trying to convey her surprise about the whole thing.

"I think he felt rather guilty about my having fainted, Mrs. Miller, that is all," Mary told the white lie, really not knowing what else she should do. After all, she simply could not tell her friend the truth of what had happened. She had sworn confidence to the Earl, and she intended to keep it.

"You mean he came in here in all that state simply because you fainted away before him?" Mrs. Miller was chuckling. "Men, they can be strange sometimes!"

Mary felt terrible about the need to lie to her friend and decided to pepper her lies with a few truths.

"It was a little more than that, I'm afraid, Mrs. Miller." Mary smiled somewhat confidentially. "You see, we had just begun another one of our truly momentous arguments in the moments before I fainted."

"Goodness me! Not Miss Morgan again?" Mrs. Miller's eyes were wide in astonishment. "Because the Earl was most insistent that Daisy looks after the twins until you were better. Not just through the day, mind you, but early mornings and evenings too, no less!"

"No, not Miss Morgan this time. Although, I have to say, I am rather glad that he finally heeded my words and has developed some misgivings of his own regarding the nurse."

"So, he realizes that Miss Morgan's reports of bad behavior have been somewhat over exaggerated then?" Mrs. Miller went delightfully off-track, and Mary smiled, feeling the warmth and comfort which so often accompanied their conversations somehow seeping into her very heart and making her feel so much better.

"You know, I believe he is starting to see it. And I cannot tell you how relieved I am to know that Daisy has them with her."

"Oh, they are having a wonderful time with Daisy. They have begged her to show them how to do some of the cleaning duties she performs if you can believe that! So Daisy is wandering around Linwood Hall polishing everything in sight, sometimes twice!" Mrs. Miller's smile was a real treat. "They really are lovely little children, Miss Porter."

"Yes, they are coming on so well."

"As is their father," Miss Miller said with a sly grin.

"How so?"

"Well, I have seen him on more than one occasion creeping

about and watching the children as they are playing with Daisy. He seems to be lurking rather a lot, and I'm pleased to report that their adorable antics are putting secret little smiles on his face now and again."

"That is wonderful news, Mrs. Miller."

"But sadly, not the end of the story. The Earl looks rather troubled about something the rest of the time. I must say, that once or twice, the look on his face has rather led me to wonder what it is."

"Oh, dear!" Mary was beginning to panic a little; they were on dangerous ground, and she knew it. She knew that she should say nothing which would give any hint that she knew what the problem was. "I suppose that during all of his watching of the children, he has not actually approached them?"

"No, not once," Mrs. Miller said. Mary felt rather relieved, as the response had given her a way out.

"Ah, then, I daresay that his troubled expression might well be on account of the fact that he, as yet, does not know *how* to approach his children. Or how to heal the rift between them. If he's starting to find his way back to the world, I have no doubt that he shall have some rickety bridges to cross."

"Oh, you really do make so much sense, my dear. Of course, that must be it." Mrs. Miller smiled, and Mary was truly relieved to see that the danger seemed to have passed. "Oh, I almost forgot! What was it that you and the Earl were arguing about before you fell into a faint?"

"The children had gone into his study and taken some papers whilst I was asleep. You see, I felt rather dreadful as the day wore on, and I had rather nodded off in my chair. Anyway, the papers which the children had taken from the study were, in fact, documents and correspondence. Not only that but by the time I woke up again, they had drawn on a good deal of them. When the Earl had realized that much of his paperwork was missing, he came thundering along to the schoolroom and rather lost his temper when he saw the children drawing on them. In truth, he had not realized until that moment that I'd been feeling unwell, so I have rather forgiven him for it. So, you see, by the time we had started to argue about the subject, the infection really had taken hold of me, and I remember very little else."

"Well, no wonder he felt so guilty!" Mrs. Miller said, her eyes rolling up towards the heavens. "And that makes so much more sense of his sitting in here watching over you. Really, I had wondered what on earth was going on."

"Guilt is a great motivator, Mrs. Miller." Both women began to laugh.

"Anyway, more importantly, how are you feeling now, Miss Porter?"

"Oh, very much better, I thank you. I awoke with a tremendous headache, but his Lordship mixed up some of the morphine which the doctor left behind."

"Oh, that was good of him. Tell me, did he mix up any of the other preparations from the table?"

"No, I have only had the morphine."

"Then I shall prepare the other medications whilst I'm here. The doctor said it is very important that you take them all, even if you begin to improve. He said there is a very much better chance of keeping the infection from returning if you take all of his preparations as directed." Mrs. Miller bustled her way to the side table and began, rather expertly, to prepare the assorted tonics.

Once Mary had taken them all, she began to feel rather tired.

"I think I might have a little sleep, Mrs. Miller."

"Then I shall leave you for a little while, my dear, but should you like me to send you one of the maids to sit with you while you sleep?"

"No, I am feeling so much better, Mrs. Miller, that that shan't be necessary. But I should be most grateful for a fresh jug of water for washing," Mary asked, a little shyly.

"Of course, I shall send one of the girls up immediately." Mrs. Miller made her way to the wardrobe and opened it. "And here, I shall lay out a fresh nightgown for you also."

"Oh, how very kind of you, Mrs. Miller."

"Think nothing of it, Miss Porter." Mrs. Miller began to make her way to the door. "It's rather late now, so I daresay that you shall sleep nicely through the night with all of the medication. I shall pop up first thing in the morning, and we shall have a nice pot of tea together, as usual."

"Oh, that would be lovely, Mrs. Miller," Mary said, quite truthfully.

AFTER THE MAID had fetched a pleasingly warm jug of water, Mary quietly turned the key in the lock of her bedroom door. She had no idea when the Earl would be returning to tell her the rest of his story, and would much rather he did not find her in the middle of her ablutions.

As much as she had felt so much better, her wash had improved her sense of well-being tenfold. Once she had finished and had put on the fresh, crisp white nightgown, Mary sat at her dressing table and spent some minutes brushing her thick brown hair. Happy that she had brushed it to a shine, Mary swept her thick tresses to one side and deftly wove them into a thick and neat plait. Leaning in towards the mirror to peer at her complexion, Mary could see just exactly how exhausted she looked. The illness had certainly taken its toll on her. Her cheeks were sunken, and she had rather dark circles about her eyes. With a sigh, Mary rose and quietly unlocked her bedroom door again before putting herself back to bed.

With no idea when the Earl might return to her, Mary decided to give in to the sleep which was so keen to pull her down into its comfortable depths.

MARY AWOKE with a start sometime later. Hearing someone at the door, Mary stared about her, but the room was in complete darkness, and she felt momentarily confused. As the door opened fully, Mary could see the light from a single candle, yet could not see who was holding it.

"I am sorry to come to you in the middle of the night, Miss Porter. Are you awake?" As he closed the door and quietly locked it behind him, the Earl began to approach her, speaking in a whisper. "In truth, I could not find a safer time to return to you."

"Oh, please, do not make yourself uneasy about it, Your Lordship. Pray, do take a seat."

Mary sat up on the bed once more, although this time she

arranged herself. In truth, the few hours' sleep she had taken had made her feel very much better, and certainly strong enough to rearrange her own pillows.

The Earl placed the candle upon her bedside table, and suddenly she could see him very much more clearly. He looked rather informal with breeches and a shirt, but his waistcoat was not done up, and he wore no necktie. Still, it was the middle of the night, and she certainly did not expect him to be dressed for dinner.

"Miss Porter, I should very much like to tell you the remainder of my tale, if you would hear it. I find that I cannot sleep a wink, and rather think that if I say it all out loud to another person, that I might be able to settle upon some course of action and finally gain some peace."

"Of course you may, Your Lordship."

"You asked me what possible proof my wife could have as to the question of my parentage. Indeed, as far as I am aware, my mother never had an affair of any kind. But in truth, that is not the point my wife is trying to make."

"Oh?" Mary could make no sense of his comment, and it was rather obvious from the tone of her voice.

"You see, Miss Porter, my mother died many years ago. I was but a child at the time, only three-years-old in fact, and I have absolutely no memory of her whatsoever."

"I'm terribly sorry to hear that, Your Lordship. I lost my mother also, but in truth, I can recollect her, and that is a great comfort to me." Mary did not really know why she had told him such a thing, except that she had, perhaps, been trying to encourage him with a private confidence of her own.

"It is a terrible thing to lose one's mother. I often think of my children, and wonder if the fact that their mother *chose* to leave them will one day have a terrible effect on them," he said, the sadness in his voice all too clear. "Anyway, as I began to get a little older, my father told me that my mother had died in Italy. The three of us had been there on a holiday; my father, mother, and me. We had apparently been there for several weeks when my mother became ill with an infectious fever which was sweeping the small town we were staying in."

"Oh, dear me." Mary rather knew what was coming next.

"And, as you rightly perceive, Miss Porter, my mother died out in Italy. After her funeral, my father returned home to Linwood with me and set about rebuilding his life. I know that he loved her terribly, for he never took another wife, and could never speak about my mother without the merest touch of a tear in his eye." The Earl paused for a few moments.

"As sad as their parting was, it sounds as if your mother and father had known true love." Although Mary did not really know what to say, when she spoke the words, they had come from her very heart.

"I believe just about the same thing, Miss Porter. In fact, I rather wonder if I shall ever experience something the same myself one day." The Earl paused to stretch his legs out in front of him.

Mary found herself fixated upon the idea that the Earl had not *truly* loved his wife. Whilst he seemed to be terribly affected by her disappearance, was it possible that hurt could be caused by anything less than the deepest of love? Mary began to think that perhaps it was.

"Anyway, by the time my father returned with me, we had been away from Linwood Hall some six months, and I myself remember nothing of that time."

"But still I do not understand how Lady Pennington can be suggesting that you are not your father's son. I'm still very much confused, Your Lordship."

"My wife states that our old Butler, George Carlton, rather told her something when he had taken one too many drinks. It must have been *more* than two years ago because the dear man passed away two years ago this month." The Earl seemed to be sadly reminded of the loss of a much cared for servant. "Constance claims that Carlton told her that the child that my father returned from Italy with was not the same child he had taken with him six months beforehand."

"What?" Mary leaned forward, suddenly aware of her rather rough exclamation.

"Apparently, Carlton told Constance that my father, almost as soon as he had returned home, had sought him out to confide in him. You see, Carlton told her that my father said that, not only had his wife died in Italy but that his son had caught the infection and died also. So you see, Miss Porter, you are talking to a ghost."

"But if your father had truly lost his child in Italy, then who is the child he is alleged to have come back with?" Mary felt she could see many flaws in Lady Pennington's rotten plan.

"According to Carlton's tale, I am an Italian orphan. My father, unable to deal with such complete loss and grief, is said to have attended one of the local orphanages and taken away a boy of the same age as the one he lost."

As the Earl sat back in his chair, seemingly exhausted, Mary thought about all she had been told. In truth, the tale might well be very plausible. It was certainly not beyond the realms of possibility that a man almost swallowed whole by grief would do something, anything, to ease his pain.

"Forgive me for saying, Your Lordship, but you are rather fair and blue-eyed for an Italian," Mary said, suddenly pleased with herself.

"I don't think that is entirely unheard of in Italy, Miss Porter," the Earl said, somewhat defeated by it all.

"Not impossible, that's true. But rather uncommon, nonetheless." Mary continued to mull it all over. "Another thing that troubles me, Your Lordship, is the question of the Butler, George Carlton. For your father to have allegedly confided in him so completely, he must really have thought him to be a man whose standards were of the highest, and whose confidence could not be breached. And yet, years later, he tells everything to your wife; a woman who had not been at Linwood Hall for very long at all. Does that not seem a little unusual to you?"

"Not entirely, I'm afraid. It's true that George Carlton was one of the finest men my father had ever known. In truth, they were great friends. But sadly, Carlton lost his wife a few years back, and from that moment on, his grief was so raw that he turned to drink. I kept him on here, obviously, but he was not able to function in exactly the same way as he always had. The drink, you see, really did have him in its wicked grasp."

"Oh, dear," Mary said, somewhat vaguely.

"Add to that the fact that my wife can be extremely charming. There is no doubt in my mind that Constance would have been digging for secrets. She was just that sort of woman, although I had not perceived that part of her nature until we had been married a little while. She was rather a devious creature, you see. Anyway, she is almost chameleon-like in her personality, and had doubtless been using her charm upon the poor old boy for some time."

"Oh, how dreadful," Mary exclaimed. Lord Pennington really was telling her everything. In just a matter of a few short hours, they had gone from quiet adversaries to the closest of confidants. If Mary had not felt so very much better, she would truly have put the change in their circumstances down to hallucination.

"I'm rather afraid that a woman who would bribe her own husband without a moment's compunction would, in truth, stick at nothing. That is the worst of it all, you see, I truly believe that she will carry out her threat." The Earl seemed to sag in his seat and let out a terrible sigh. In it, Mary could hear almost complete resignation and found that she could barely stand it. What an appalling way for a decent man to be treated. And not just *any* man, but the woman's own husband... the man with whom she had created two beautiful children. Whatever sort of a monster was Lady Constance Pennington?

"Right, then let's be practical, Your Lordship." Mary was suddenly determined to do whatever she could to help him. "If the story Lady Pennington is telling is anything close to the truth, let us think of how it is she could possibly prove it."

"Oh, right." The Earl straightened up in his seat, and once more Mary was reminded of the unruly child she had managed to tame at her Dame school. Perhaps she was destined to speak to everybody in the style of a governess. Her father would certainly have agreed, she thought with an internal smile.

"First of all, if we assume that Lady Pennington is still in the company of the Count, what part of Italy would that put her in?"

"Count Costanzo lives in the very heart of Turin."

"And do you know in which area your family was taking their holiday all those years ago?"

"My father always said it was Moncalieri."

"Which is where, in relation to Turin?"

"It is but a few miles outside. Maybe five, or six?"

Mary felt rather a sinking feeling. If the woman was so close to the area in which the young Emerson Rutherford was alleged to have died, perhaps she already had the information she needed.

"Rather a little too close for comfort, is it not?" It seemed that the Earl had come to the same conclusions that she had herself.

"It *is* close, Your Lordship, but it is equally likely to be a simple coincidence."

"Perhaps." Mary could sense that she was losing him again. She had boosted his spirits with a promise of action and felt that she had rather failed in her quest.

"So, assuming Lady Pennington begins to make inquiries in the Moncalieri area, what is she likely to be looking for?" Mary went on, bravely.

"Perhaps she will petition the local orphanages. Maybe she is hoping to find certain paperwork in relation to an adoption of some kind."

"What year would it have been, Your Lordship?" Mary rather

gathered that the Earl was older than her, but did not entirely know by how much.

"Well, let me think. I was three-years-old at the time, and I am thirty-three years old now, so it would have been in the year 1795," Emerson said, squinting somewhat at the rather simple arithmetic.

"In truth, I'm not entirely sure how well-kept records of such things truly are. Even in this country, and even in this year, I do not know how stringent the requirements are. In a small town outside of Turin, some thirty years ago, there might very well have been no paperwork completed at all. And even if there had been, there is nothing to say that it would remain all these years later."

"I must say, Miss Porter, that all sounds rather promising. In truth, you have made me feel a little better, although I shall not rest entirely easy until I find a way to be at the end of all this mess." The Earl stifled a yawn; he seemed to be truly exhausted. "I still have no clue how I should proceed. I really did think that if I talked it all through with you, that I would come to some conclusion, and yet I cannot."

"That is because you have been, and still are, trying to solve the thing yourself. You really must allow me to help you, Your Lordship, for two heads are always better than one."

"I should be most grateful for your help, Miss Porter. However, you are currently unwell, and it would be too much for me to expect."

"Oh, do stop finding ways to defeat yourself! I am currently unwell, but improving all the time. I shall very soon be entirely well, and there is nothing to stop me putting some thought into the whole thing in the meantime."

For a few moments, the Earl's mouth drooped open in surprise. Suddenly realizing how dreadfully inappropriate her tone was in addressing an Earl of the Realm, Mary was glad that the light from the candle would surely not show the reddening of her cheeks.

"Oh, dear! I really am most terribly sorry, Your Lordship. I'm rather afraid I have spent far too much time in recent years dealing solely with children. Please, do forgive my insolent tone."

"Certainly, Miss Porter." Suddenly the Earl began to laugh, and rather loudly. Almost as soon as he had started, he realized that he risked being discovered in Mary's room. Hurriedly, he clamped one hand over his mouth, almost as if to swallow down his mirth. Relieved that he had not chastised her for her tone, Mary still did not quite know what to say.

In the weeks since she had arrived at Linwood Hall, Mary had been so consumed with worry for the children, and a concern that the Earl might dismiss her from her post, that she had hardly been herself. At that moment, she knew that the strident young schoolmistress, the one whom her own father had hidden from on occasion, had returned with full force. In truth, she was rather glad to see her old self again, albeit in rather embarrassing circumstances.

Once the Earl had regained his composure, he turned to address Mary once more.

"Well, now that I have told you all of it, perhaps I should allow you to sleep for a while." The Earl shifted forward in his seat, clearly displaying his intention to quit her room directly.

"Indeed, Your Lordship. But please do return tomorrow, if

you are able to. Once I've slept upon the problem, I might very well come up with a plan of some sort."

"I cannot tell you how grateful I am to have an ally in all of this, Miss Porter. Well, I shall return to you tomorrow, whenever I see a clear chance."

"In the meantime, Your Lordship, please do have a very good think about what you remember from your own childhood. In particular, try to think what your earliest memories are. You never know, you might come up with something which helps to dispel the story entirely."

"Or prove it," he said, but with none of the tone of resignation she had previously perceived in his voice.

"Whatever it proves or disproves, Your Lordship, I rather think that the starting point of all shall be the truth. It rather strikes me that the truth shall be all-important."

CHAPTER 9

*M*ary awoke much earlier than she would have liked the following morning. It was only six o'clock, and she knew fine well that Mrs. Miller would certainly not be arriving with their morning tea much before seven. Mary tried pointlessly for another half an hour of sleep, and yet her brain was darting to and fro and would not let her return to her slumber.

In truth, it was not simply the Earl's strange and convoluted secret which had made her mind so alert so very early in the morning. The sudden, seismic shift in their relationship had Mary rather reeling in shock. Lord Pennington's very act of confiding in her, especially in the middle of the night and by candlelight, had seemed to Mary to be so very intimate. For one thing, Mary had never been alone in a bedroom with a man in her life, and even though the proceedings had been quite innocent, still she felt a tiny thrill of pleasure at the thought of it.

Furthermore, the very nature of the secret he had told her

had the potential to be extremely damaging to him. Even more than damaging, it truly threatened to end his world as he knew it. Mary could hardly believe he had trusted her with its knowledge.

The more she thought about Lord Pennington and everything he had endured, the more she began to see how easy it might be to lose sight of what was important. It was clear that the Earl had some idea of Lady Pennington's true nature, even before she had run away with the Count.

Mary thought what a dreadful thing it must be to discover that one's spouse was not who one thought they were. Especially after you had brought children into the world together.

Still, there were elements of the whole thing which somehow warmed her heart. If Lord Pennington could open up in the way that he had with Mary, then there was great hope for his future relationship with Oliver and Isobel. After weeks of wondering and worrying, Mary felt a real hope that the tiny family could be saved. However, she really rather hoped the family would not be saved, only to be lost again. If Lady Pennington's assertions were true and, worse, if she could indeed prove them, then the Earl and his children would undoubtedly suffer for many years to come. If not for the rest of their lives.

Picturing the angelic little faces of Oliver and Isobel, Mary rather determined to do everything in her power to help their father reach a proper conclusion to the matter. The idea that the twins would ever return to the shy and confused creatures they had been when she had arrived was something that Mary simply could not bear.

Somewhat more disconcertingly, Mary found herself picturing the handsome face of Oliver and Isobel's father. Rather surprisingly, Mary found that the idea of the Earl suffering any more than he had done already was equally unbearable to her. In the last few hours, Mary knew that she and Lord Pennington had made a very real connection, and the truth of it was that Mary already began to feel that connection very deeply.

* * *

ALTHOUGH HE HAD SLEPT for only four or five hours, Emerson realized that it was the longest sleep he had managed for many days. Ordinarily, he would have felt truly dreadful on such little sleep. Yet, as he awoke on the morning after he had unburdened himself to Mary Porter, he rather strangely felt better than he had done for a very long time.

Although they had yet to come up with a firm plan of action, Emerson felt vastly more optimistic about the whole thing than he had done previously. There was something about Mary Porter's rather strident tone and attitude which seemed somehow to inspire confidence.

Even as he was still relating the dreadful tale, Mary seemed to be constantly thinking. In truth, she had come up with much that he might well have decided for himself had he not been so truly exhausted and worried. Mary had said that two heads were better than one, and as far as Emerson was concerned, she had been most certainly right about that.

From the very moment of waking, Emerson had racked his brains for thoughts of his childhood, doing whatever he could to remember his life as a three-year-old boy. In truth, there was very little that he could remember, and his attempts were intermittently hampered by unbidden thoughts of Mary Porter.

From the moment he had interviewed her, Emerson had known her to be a very beautiful woman. However, his recent experiences had rather soured him against the female of the species, and Mary Porter had fared no better than any other woman in his field of vision.

He knew that it wasn't simply that she had listened to him which had made him finally sit up and take notice. Rather, it was the moment she had collapsed, white faced and obviously desperately ill, when he realized what she had quietly, almost silently, come to mean to him.

When they had first argued about the children and Miss Morgan, Emerson had known then what a sensible woman she was. Her strength and resolve showed how much she had already come to care for his children. Furthermore, Mary had proven herself to be brave on that day, for she had not only called a *father* to account but an *Earl.*

Even whilst he had angrily raged against her, Emerson had known that she had spoken the truth. In the very moment that he had effectively fired her, Emerson knew that he really did not want to let her go. Mary Porter had not been run-of-the-mill; rather, she was quite simply unlike any other woman he had ever met.

On that day when she had told him that she had money of her own and no need to work, Emerson had been entirely baffled by her ambivalence to her own wealth. It had taken him some time to realize that, for Mary, teaching was the type of work which had value in itself, and value beyond monetary payment.

In the many weeks that she had worked at Linwood Hall,

Emerson had rather come to know Mary by stealth. Unable to admit to himself that Mary Porter had interested him in any way, Emerson had found himself listening at the door of the schoolroom as she engaged with his children. Sometimes, he would find himself peering out of windows to watch her out on the tiny flower bed as Oliver and Isobel had planted their haphazard little arrangements. Emerson smiled to himself as he thought of the dreadful chaos and colors which his children's gardening had created. It was clear that Mary had not in any way interfered, nor tried to impose an adult's sense of order and neatness to their work. Rather she had left them to their own imaginations, simply helping them where they needed it, but otherwise allowing true learning to take place.

Finally, Emerson had come to admit to himself that he rather liked Miss Porter, and had determined to learn something more about her. However, almost on the very day that he had decided to seek her out for conversation, the dreadful letter had arrived in the first post.

In that terrible moment when he had found his office desk empty of paperwork, and had run into the schoolroom, he had known that the paper in Mary's hand would undoubtedly be that letter. He had felt as though his world had suddenly begun to fall in upon itself, and had no notion whatsoever at the time that Mary's knowledge of the letter would be the best thing that could possibly have happened.

* * *

EMERSON HAD ARRIVED in Mary's room soon after Mrs. Miller had departed. He had waited until he saw his housekeeper leave before making his way in, judging it to be a time in which he was unlikely to be found in Mary's room.

After all, Mrs. Miller was unlikely to return for some time and, it being so early in the morning still, the rest of the household were sure to be busy with their own work.

"Did you have any chance, Your Lordship, to think back over your childhood at all since I saw you last?" No sooner had Emerson enquired after her health than Mary had returned to the idea of solving his terrible problem.

"I have been thinking about it since I awoke this morning, and can tell you this; try as I might, I have absolutely no recollection of my mother whatsoever. I realize that I was only three-years-old at the time, but still, I should have thought there would be something, a vague impression of another person in my life."

"I really am not sure if that is the case. Perhaps such a young child is more prone to forget." Mary could not help but try to soothe him a little.

"I *would* that were true, if only for the sake of my own children." The sudden look of sadness on his face gave Mary the most dreadful pang of sympathy for him. Not only him but the children also.

"Still, if you can remember nothing at all of that age, then perhaps it is simply natural that you cannot recall your mother."

"Ah, but I *do* remember something," Emerson said, casting his eyes down just for a moment.

"Really?" Mary could hear a certain trepidation in her own voice.

"Yes, believe it or not, I rather think that I remember something of the journey home to England. It's nothing specific, you see, and yet I have an impression of it. I have the idea of being on board a ship, and for several days. I also have a notion of my father being there, although I cannot entirely trust my recollections on that particular point. In truth, I daresay that I cannot trust my recollections on any point which goes back thirty years."

"Although your recollection of that journey neither proves nor disproves what Lady Pennington is alleging, it still rather feels like progress of a sort." Mary chewed thoughtfully at her bottom lip, staring out into space. She was both surprised and grateful that the Earl had not interrupted her silent thought process.

"Your Lordship, is there anyone in your household now who was also in your household back then?" Mary asked, quite suddenly.

"I'm afraid not, Miss Porter. George Carlton was the last of them."

"And any family in the area at the time whom you could rely upon now to speak the truth?"

"Again, no. My father was an only child, and I have no knowledge of my mother's family. I do not have any direct cousins, but very distant ones descended from my father's own aunts and uncles. I'm afraid my father and I led rather a solitary life. He had very few friends that I remember, and certainly none who were regular visitors to Linwood. I have never really thought about it before, except to attribute my own taciturn nature to that style of living." Emerson smiled sadly and gave a shrug of his shoulders.

Mary was lost in thought once more, sadly thinking of the little boy he must once have been, all alone in such an enormous house with his heartbroken father.

"So, no remaining servants, no close family, and no visiting friends." Mary was speaking quietly, almost to herself. "You had a nurse, surely?"

"Indeed. In fact, my first nurse is one of my earliest memories. And she most certainly would have arrived *after* we had returned from Italy because I have a very good impression of my father taking me to her for the first time. Before that, I do not know if I had a nurse. My father never spoke of it, and I never really thought of it, I suppose I rather assumed that my mother had looked after me herself. Of course, if I was, indeed, an Italian orphan, then the fact that I only remember having a nurse after my return from Italy would certainly apply, wouldn't it?"

"Indeed, it *could* apply." Mary did not want to do him the disservice of sugar coating everything, and at the same time, she did not want to beat him with a reality that might well prove to be true. "Were there any professionals or other workmen who visited the house regularly during your childhood? Anyone at all?" Mary had the awful feeling that she was clutching at straws. This little family seemed to have resided in quiet self-sufficiency for two generations, and it all rather left her with very little by way of clues.

"Apart from our Doctor, no, I can't think of……" Emerson sat bolt upright in his chair. "Of course! That's it! The doctor who tended to my father and me for as long as I can remember was probably the most regular visitor we had. My father, it has to be said, saw him rather regularly. Although, in truth, I never really knew what was ailing him. Anyway, I remember Dr. Philpott as far back as I remember my first nurse. In truth, there is a very good chance that he will have attended me my whole life. From the moment I was born, in fact."

"And is he still….?"

"Alive? Yes, I haven't seen him for years, but I'm certain that he's still alive. I have never heard anything to the contrary, at any rate. He retired from practice when I was about sixteen years of age. I daresay, if I am right in assuming that he still lives, then Dr. Philpott would certainly be well into his eighties by now."

"And he stayed in the area?" Mary was also sitting bolt upright, suddenly rather excited at the prospect of making progress.

"I believe that he did! In truth, it is years since I have seen him, or even thought about him, if I'm honest. Still, it's just a matter of a few inquiries to find out for sure. In fact, I am quite certain that I could find out all we need to know before today is quite over."

"Now, that is progress, Your Lordship. I really must congratulate you."

"Let us hope that he is alive and well and living nearby." Emerson was smiling broadly at her. "And if he is all of those things, let us hope that he is still in possession of his wits."

"Your Lordship!" Mary could not help but laugh, whilst shaking her head slowly from side to side in the style of a lifelong governess.

"Perhaps, if you do not mind, you could call me Emerson," he said, his sudden shyness making him suddenly appear many years younger.

"Oh, I don't know… Your Lordship…" Mary was extremely flustered, and it showed.

"I should esteem it a great favor, Miss Porter. You see, I very seldom hear my Christian name spoken aloud. You have no doubt perceived that I live a very solitary life here, and I am surrounded by people who call me *My Lord* or *Your Lordship*. When I am away from home, the people I meet call me *Earl* or *Lord Pennington*. In truth, I should very much like to hear my name spoken from time to time."

"I can understand that entirely. I had not realized until this moment, but I have not heard my own name uttered since I last met up with my father." Even though Mary had seen her father most Sundays since she had moved to Linwood Hall, still she felt the sudden deprivation of that closeness. For some moments, she tried to imagine what it would feel like to hear your own name spoken so very rarely, if at all.

"Well, when there is nobody else around, I should be very glad to call you Emerson. And I must insist then that you call me Mary, and return me the same favor."

"I should like that, Mary." Emerson seemed an equal mixture of pleased and embarrassed to be calling Mary by her Christian name. Something about his manner suddenly made him look like a much younger man again.

"So, if we find that Dr. Philpott is still in the area, will you go to see him?" Mary said, keen to know what the next step might be.

"I think I must." Emerson seemed to contemplate for a few moments. "But I should very much like it if you came with me. As I remember, old Dr. Philpott responded rather well to pretty young ladies. He attended one or two of the female servants in the past, and I rather have a recollection of his ability to make even the most unwell of women rather chuckle."

"Well, if you are happy for me to be there, I should be very glad to go with you, Emerson." Mary felt her cheeks flush a little, as she self-consciously spoke his name.

"Then it is settled. I shall do what I can to locate Dr. Philpott and, as soon as you are well and able, if he is still living, we shall go to see him."

CHAPTER 10

*M*ary and Emerson rode to the outskirts of Linwood town in near silence. Ever since Emerson had discovered the whereabouts of Dr. Philpott, Mary had nursed a silent worry that the elderly Doctor might very well not remember the previous Earl of Pennington and his young son, Emerson. Although she was beginning to formulate some ideas of her own as to how they should proceed, finding out the truth of the allegation one way or the other would certainly help.

"I do hope he still has his memories," Emerson said, suddenly breaking the silence.

Emerson had been quiet all morning. Whilst their trip to Doctor Philpott had still been in the planning stage, he had seemed rather more hopeful. When he had returned to Mary's room with the news that Doctor Philpott was not only still alive, but still in the area, Emerson had been rather jubilant. He had gathered the information in just a matter of hours and had been so keen to tell Mary of his progress that he was almost caught by a housemaid striding into her bedroom.

Mary's mood had been strangely affected by Emerson's, and she found that she, too, had been very high-spirited upon finding out that the elderly Doctor was still in the area.

Mary herself had decided that they must go the very next morning. Although she was feeling very much better, Emerson was concerned that the trip out of doors so early into her recovery might very well cause a physical setback of some kind. However, Mary had been so determined that, in the end, the Earl gave into her.

"I have been thinking the very same thing, Emerson. Everything felt so hopeful yesterday, and now I simply feel nervous," Mary said.

"Yes, and I'm rather afraid I feel the same. I cannot help but think that a man so far into his eighties, and who retired so many years ago, is likely to be nowhere near as sharp as he once was."

"And yet, he might be. I think our nerves are getting the better of us both, and we are creating catastrophes before we even know if they exist."

"Yes, I think you're right." Emerson laughed for the first time that morning.

Feeling increasingly comfortable in his company, Mary felt at liberty to study him just a little longer than she ordinarily might have done. Every time he laughed, Emerson's face was completely transformed. Always a handsome man, there was something so very appealing about him when he was laughing. Again, she found herself looking at his skin, hair, and eyes. He wasn't pale by any stretch of the imagination, but he most certainly was not dark. Although his hair was light brown, with flecks of blond, it would most likely have been very much paler when he was a child. His skin was tanned because he spent so much time out of doors, wandering the grounds of the estate or riding out across the countryside. If he had been more of an indoor man, he would certainly have been a lot paler.

And yet, in spite of it all, Mary still had the most terrible misgivings. Not everybody in Italy had dark hair and dark eyes, even if it was rather more common. Furthermore, she could not begin to imagine that Lady Pennington had made the entire thing up. After all, if she was making it up, there could be no proof for her to find, and the entire thing would be a foolish waste of time. Unless, of course, Emerson chose simply to pay her at her first request. Then, of course, it would simply have been a rather cleverly played confidence trick.

Mary knew that she was going around and round in circles and that thoughts which tended in either direction did little to help.

"I say, Mary. It's rather a strange thing, but I have to admit that I am afraid that Dr. Philpott will remember *nothing* and equally afraid that he will remember *everything.*"

"Yes, I can understand that very well. And it is perfectly human; you need the truth in order to continue, and yet the truth might very well be painful."

"Yes, Mary, I believe that is true." Emerson seemed to have settled into a quiet contemplation once more.

"But much apart from needing the truth in order to be able to plan your next move in this business with Lady Pennington, I rather think there is something more important here. You see, in the end, we all need to know who we are. Wherever that leads us, and whatever the outcome, the truth of who we are is a most fundamental thing."

"Yes, I suppose it is. The problem is, I am rather afraid to find out."

"Yes, I understand."

"Because, you see, there was only ever my father and I. All these years, I had assumed, without thinking, that he must have loved me."

"And you think if we discover that, after all, he was *not* your father, that he did not love you at all?" Mary looked over at Emerson, who did not respond but simply looked back at her. "Emerson, whatever the outcome of this, the man you thought of as your father *was* your father. If you did, indeed, hail from an orphanage in Italy, then the man you have always called *father* chose you to be his son. From everything you say about him, if you were not truly his child, it would seem to me that he made no distinction. If *he* made no distinction, then I think perhaps that *you* should not either. To sire a child is one thing, and to raise one is quite another. It is the raising of a child that is important, and the raising of the child which earns the title of *Father or Mother*. The rest is, quite simply, biology."

Emerson seemed to think very deeply about everything Mary had said. His eyebrows knitted together in thought, and he had leaned forward on the carriage seat, resting his elbows on his knees, and his face in his hands. For the entire time, he kept his eyes on Mary's.

"You know, Mary, you really are most very sensible and very caring. And at the same time, you manage to be rather blunt and clinical." Seeing Mary purse her lips, the Earl began to laugh. "And I really, genuinely, think you managed to fit every facet of your personality into your last sentence. I really do not know how you do it." His laughing had increased in intensity and to a point where Mary could not possibly be offended by what he had said, only amused.

"I am rather afraid that my own father would agree with you on the matter of my bluntness. He has been attempting to chastise me for it since I was a little child."

"And did he make any progress?"

"I am rather afraid that his struggle continues." Mary smiled at him, and Emerson reached across and lightly patted her hand.

"Oh, I say! I think we are here, Mary."

Mary looked into his face with a smile of encouragement as the carriage slowly drew to a halt. Her stomach felt as though it was full of tiny birds, all flapping hard for freedom. There was a slight tightness in her throat, and she felt a little nauseous. Mary rather hoped that it was not, indeed, a return of her illness. However, she knew herself well enough to know that this dreadful feeling was, in fact, nerves.

THE DOOR WAS VERY QUICKLY ANSWERED by a tall and thin woman in an austere black dress and a stiff, immaculate white apron. She was in her mid-forties, and Mary wondered if she was the housekeeper, or if she could possibly be the doctor's daughter. The woman had a most serious expression and rather frowned at Mary and Emerson as if they had interrupted her in her work, and she would never be able to catch up.

"Good morning. I'm sorry to trouble you, but I was

wondering if it would be possible to speak with Dr. Philpott for a few moments," Emerson said with such a charming smile that Mary was rather taken aback. Despite holding himself as something of a recluse, it very much seemed to Mary that Emerson could have charmed the birds from the trees with a look like that, and she rather wondered how a man who kept very much to himself had learned to do such a thing.

"I'm sure that won't be a problem, Sir. May I ask who is calling?" The woman's entire demeanor had changed. Suddenly, whatever work she had been doing before they arrived, clearly no longer mattered to her. Mary had to bite her tongue to stop herself from chuckling.

"I am Lord Pennington, madam, and this is my friend, Mary Porter."

The sudden blandishment of his title would certainly have sealed the deal, had the good woman not already been so very impressed with his charming smile.

"Please do come in, Your Lordship." The woman smiled at him, ignoring Mary entirely. "If you would kindly take a seat here in the hall, I will see if Dr. Philpott is available for visitors."

Mary and Emerson silently took seats in the neat, but sparsely furnished, hallway. The house was of a good size, with a very reasonable plot of land, and just far enough out of town for it to be rather more rural in setting.

Mary cast a look at Emerson, but could not read his expression at all. In truth, she knew that he must be suffering the most terrible sort of apprehension possible. Quite possibly, the next few moments might decide for him *exactly* who he was. He might be who he had always thought he was, and he might not. At that moment, Mary could think of nothing to say to him which would bring him comfort. Perhaps, in such circumstances, there is no such thing as comfort.

"Dr. Philpott is in the library if you'd like to follow me." The smiling housekeeper was back. Mary had decided since the woman had not described their host as anything other than Dr. Philpott, that she was not very likely to be his daughter. "I shall bring some tea in directly."

Mary and Emerson rose to their feet, and slowly began to follow in the housekeeper's wake. Mary felt a stab of annoyance with herself; her heart was thundering in her chest, and her palms had begun to sweat. In some respects, she felt she had no right to such feelings since the whole thing was entirely Emerson Rutherford's ordeal. And yet, the feeling persisted. In truth, Mary could not bear to see the man she had finally come to know as a *good* man, being hurt.

"I say! Well, I don't know how many years it has been!" Dr. Philpott rose quite easily from his armchair as Emerson and Mary entered the room. The man was clearly elderly, with white hair, wrinkly skin, and a vaguely stooped bearing. And yet, at the same time, as he strode across the room to greet them, Mary could not help but think how very mobile and vital the man seemed to be. His eyes seemed to sparkle and were of an amazingly beautiful blue hue. He fixed them most decidedly upon Mary and treated her to a rather lopsided grin. Holding out a hand, he introduced himself to Mary first, and she could quite see what the Earl had been talking about when he'd said that the doctor had always had a special way with young ladies.

"Well, I'm sure you already know that I am Dr. Marston Philpott, and I'm very pleased to meet you, Miss...?" The doctor held firmly to her hand throughout the entire introduction, and Mary felt an almost instant like for him.

"I am Mary Porter, Dr. Philpott, and I am very pleased to meet you also." Mary could feel her face being pulled into a huge and somewhat inevitable smile. He really was a lovely old thing. "I am the governess to Lord Pennington's two children, Sir."

"Oh, yes, of course! I had heard that you had become a father, Lord Pennington. And how does that suit you, my boy?" Dr. Philpott gently turned his attention away from Mary and settled it upon Emerson.

Mary could see the genuine warmth in Emerson's countenance and rather guessed that he had always had a fondness for the doctor. She also rather enjoyed hearing the Earl of Pennington being described as *my boy*. No doubt an old habit from years of treating the man before him when he was, indeed, a child.

"I suppose I ought to say that it has its ups and downs, Dr. Philpott," Emerson said.

Mary was rather pleased that he did not patronize the old man by telling him that parenthood was rosy. "Of course, I am rather raising them without a mother."

"Yes, I had heard something about that. Whatever happened there, I am most terribly sorry, my boy. Still, your father did the whole thing alone, and he did rather a good job by the looks of you. So, there's no reason why you can't do the same, eh?"

"No, indeed! You make a very good point, Doctor." Emerson was laughing.

There was just something about this dear old man that Mary

found rather raised one's spirits. He struck her as being rather kindly and extremely jolly and fun; the sort of grandfather she'd always wished for.

"Now, come on in and let's take a seat. I'm eighty-seven, you know, and I cannot stand all day long." He addressed the last to Mary, complete with a little wink. Mary watched the doctor stride back to his seat like a man in his sixties and rather thought that he could have stayed on his feet for a good part of the day if he had needed to. He really was such a gem of a character that Mary almost forgot their reason for being there. In truth, she could have chatted happily to the lovely old man all day, never once striking the subject of Emerson's parentage.

"I'd say you look awfully well for a man of eighty-seven, Dr. Philpott," Emerson began. "In fact, you don't seem to have aged a great deal since we last met."

"You flatter me, my boy!"

"No, indeed! Yes, your hair is white, and you have a wrinkle or two more than you used to have, but your bearing and your vitality seems rather unaltered to me. And you do not seem to have lost your eye for a pretty young lady either." Emerson finished with a warm and hearty laugh.

"I'm eighty-seven, my dear boy, not dead!" He turned to Mary and gave her a rather mischievous smile. "Never give up, that's my motto, my dear!"

Mary found herself chuckling, and knew that she had very definitely fallen under the spell of the elderly physician.

"So, what brings you to me after all these years, Emerson Rutherford?" Dr. Philpott was clearly no fool, and he had steered the conversation in the right direction where

Emerson and Mary had found themselves unable to. "It cannot be my professional opinion since I hung that up nearly twenty years ago."

"It rather is, and it isn't, I'm afraid," Emerson began, his nervousness returning. "You see, I have a question to ask you, and it is really rather awkward."

Mary felt that her mouth had suddenly gone dry, and rather wished that the housekeeper would hurry up with the tea she had promised.

"Go on, my boy," Dr. Philpott said, smiling his encouragement at Emerson.

"Well, I'm rather afraid it's a question of my origins, Dr. Philpott." The look of grim determination on Emerson's face made Mary feel most terribly sorry for him.

"Well, now, my boy. I'm afraid that I never really expected that this day would come, and I must tell you that you have caught me rather unawares." Dr. Philpott smiled kindly and rather sadly at Emerson. Mary felt a tightness in her throat so strong that she would not be able to trust herself to speak. In that simple sentence, Dr. Philpott had confirmed the Earl of Pennington's worst fears.

Before another word was spoken, the attention of all three of them was drawn by a rattling at the door, which clearly signified that the housekeeper had, indeed, kept to her promise of tea.

Not one word was spoken in the time it had taken the housekeeper to set down the tea tray, and Mary to pour them all a cup and hand them around. In some respects, Mary rather thought that had been a good thing. The housekeeper's interruption had come at exactly the right time and had given Emerson just a few moments to digest the initial shock of having his worst fears confirmed.

Once they had all taken a drink, Mary rather wished that the conversation would resume.

"So, I was not his son," Emerson said, making a statement rather than asking a question.

"No, you were not," Dr. Philpott answered, nonetheless. His kindly old eyes spoke volumes about the caring heart of the elderly physician.

"And he confided it all to you?"

"He rather had to, my boy. You see, I had been there at the birth of his son, and attended every infant illness. When he returned from Italy, I, more than anybody else would *know* that the child he returned with was not the child he had left with."

"And you challenged him upon it?"

"I didn't really have to challenge him, my boy. I could see it in his eyes, and I rather think that he always knew that I would work it out. Still, he didn't try to hide you from me, he didn't keep you out of the way for a year or two, by which time I would very likely not have been any the wiser. No, he brought you right to me. He had only been home from Italy but a few days when he brought you around to my office." Dr. Philpott's old eyes seemed intent upon a spot somewhere far in the distance, almost as if he was looking back into the past quite literally. "And that was the first out-of-the-way thing, you see. Ordinarily, I attended Linwood Hall. That the Earl had attended my office in *person* was something quite out of the ordinary. And, of course, there was not a thing wrong with you. You were as healthy as a little horse, not even so much as a sniffle. In truth, there really was no reason for him to bring you to me. I've always wondered if he rather needed somebody to confide in about it all."

"Dr. Philpott, I should be most terribly grateful if you would tell me it all. Everything he told you, leave nothing out." Emerson's expression had settled a little, and Mary rather felt a surge of pride for him. He was taking it all in, and dealing with it. Emerson Rutherford had sought knowledge of his true origins, and now he was facing the truth head-on, wanting to hear it all, however painful it might be.

"Then I shall do just that, my boy." Dr. Philpott reached for his tea as if to soothe his throat in preparation for the tale. "And I shall very much start at the beginning."

"Thank you," Emerson said.

"Firstly, I shall start by telling you that I knew your father for many years. I began my practice here as a young man, and your father was yet younger still. I watched him grow into a fine young man, and take on his responsibilities as Earl when his own father died very suddenly. I always found your father an approachable, sensible, and caring sort of man, despite being a member of the aristocracy." He gave Emerson a little smile, and Mary could have got to her feet and raced over to kiss the man. His timing was perfect, his jollity well measured, and his caring for the young man before him was obvious. Emerson chuckled quietly at the comical jibe at his class.

"And so when he married young Margaret Westbury, I couldn't have been more pleased. She was a local girl, living with her mother who was a widow. They were of steady means; neither well off nor poor, if you can see what I'm saying. Anyway, really rather an ordinary background. Still, that did not bother your father. In truth, I do not think it even occurred to him. Titles and breeding seemed to be a matter upon which he never really spoke, and he married Margaret purely and simply because he adored her."

Mary's emotions were mixed and rather confusing. She could still feel the shock of the revelation, not to mention the sadness of what surely was to follow. But there was curiosity too, and she could not help but feel a little ashamed of that.

"They really did seem wonderfully happy, and the new Lady Pennington had the constitution of an ox. Strange really, because she was rather a tiny thing. Anyway, she seemed to sail through pregnancy and childbirth, and the two of them were clearly elated when the child was born." Dr. Philpott stopped to clear his throat, and Mary rather worried if the stress of the day would have any sort of poor effect upon him. "For the first three years, they seemed to float along quite happily, much like any other young married couple with a child. Then they decided to go to Italy for a holiday. Lady Pennington had never been out of the country before, and she had been reading about Italy all her life apparently. Your father got me to give the three of them the once over before they left, just to make sure they were all fit and well. After all, they were about to spend several weeks at sea." Dr. Philpott gave an involuntary shudder and looked at Mary briefly. Clearly, he was not fond of sailing. "I knew they would be gone for some months and, beyond hoping that they had traveled safely and were enjoying their trip, I rather carried on with my business and have to admit to giving them very little thought. Anyway, some two months before your father returned, I received a rather sad letter from him. He told me of the infection which had seized Lady Pennington within a few short weeks of their arrival in Italy. As he told it to me, it had been rather something of an epidemic which had swept the little region in which they were staying, and many of the locals had died as a result. And so, despite her fine constitution, dear Margaret succumbed to the dreadful illness, and was buried in the land she had always wished to see." Dr. Philpott paused for a moment, his face a picture of sadness. His mind really was as sharp as a pin, and his memory was clearer than crystal.

As he spoke, Mary could see that he remembered Margaret Westbury well, and had clearly liked the woman very much. All these years later, the sadness of it all still had the ability to have its effects upon him.

"Which I always thought was extremely sad." He said, rather more quietly.

"My poor father," Emerson said, more to himself than to anybody else.

"Indeed, I do not know how the poor man coped with it all. He had to deal with his grief, and make his way back home, enduring several weeks of an arduous sailing, on a ship with a motherless child. I must tell you that, when I saw him again just days after his return, the Earl of Pennington was very much a changed man. I had never seen him look so thin, nor his countenance so gray. The sadness seemed almost to ooze from his pores, and permeate every space around him."

Despite her resolve not to, Mary felt her eyes welling with tears and had to blink rather hard and fast to disperse them before they fell. The very thought of losing the person you loved in a foreign country and, having buried them there, having to leave them behind, struck Mary most deeply. The poor old Earl had not even had a grave to visit. He had no place to go in which to release his appalling grief. No place to talk to his lost love.

"The moment he carried you into my office in his arms, I knew that something was not quite right. I remember it as if it happened yesterday, my boy. Your father took the fireside armchair in my office, with you on his knee. He saw my quizzical look immediately, of course, but it did not seem to stir him. Rather he just turned you around on his lap, so that I could study you entirely. He then said, and I shall never forget this as long as I draw breath, *"Well, my dear Philpott, he's a fine little fellow, is he not?"* At that moment, I knew that he was rather confessing to me. To this day, I have wondered if that was his intent all along, but I daresay I shall not know the answer to that until I myself am…" He raised his beautiful blue eyes to the heavens and then smiled warmly at them both.

"It sounds as if you were rather put on the spot, Dr. Philpott," Emerson began to reach for his already empty cup, and seeing it was so, Mary hastened to pour him another from the teapot without speaking. Dr. Philpott did not speak whilst Emerson took his drink, allowing the young man before him to slowly digest the information, piece by piece. "Whatever did you say to it all, Dr. Philpott?" Emerson continued, noisily returning his cup to the saucer.

"I said, *"Yes, he most certainly is a fine little fellow. He is not your fine little fellow, though, is he?"* In truth, I did not know what else to say."

Emerson laughed a little, and Mary rather wondered if such a response was typical of the wonderfully unflappable old doctor.

"He then told me the whole thing. Margaret had died of the dreadful infection, and he had suffered every agony of burying a young and beautiful woman whilst he cradled his little son in his arms. Then, as he had been contemplating his journey home, the little boy slowly began to show signs of the same dreadful illness. He did everything in his power to nurse the child and slept not one wink throughout the whole thing. When finally the little boy died, Lord Pennington found himself yet again arranging the funeral of a most adored family member. He told me that, in the days of waiting for that funeral to take place, he wandered the streets of Moncalieri with the horrible knowledge that he had lost everything. You see, your father had next to nobody by way of family, and his wife and child were his entire world. What should have been a wonderful experience in a beautiful foreign land had served only to rob him of the only things which had ever mattered to him. The poor man was utterly broken."

Mary had been rather surprised by the tears which had suddenly rolled down her cheeks. So intent had she been on Dr. Philpott's recitation that she had not even felt the tears forming. As quietly as she could, she opened her tiny drawstring reticule and removed a crisp, white handkerchief. As she dabbed at her eyes, she felt Emerson's gaze upon her, and she would have given anything to have been able to contain her emotions at that moment. After all, the poor man was suffering enough without having to contemplate *her* comfort.

"Mary?" Emerson reached out and gently touched her upper arm.

"I'm absolutely fine, Emerson. Please, do not make yourself worried about me." Mary successfully dried her tears and nodded at both of the men that they should continue.

"It was as your father wandered the streets of Moncalieri that he found himself one day staring in over the walls of an orphanage. It was a warm day, and several of the children had been rather left to their own devices on a small patch of lawn. At first, your father rather felt that he was seeking only to torture himself, to hammer his own loss firmly into his heart. And then he saw you. A little infant with hair as blond and eyes as blue as his own son's. He could not take his eyes from you, nor his mind from you in the days which followed. On the very day before his own son was due to be buried, your father entered that orphanage and made it very plain that he wished to take you away from there and raise you as his own child. As impoverished as all orphanages seem to be, the patrons were only too keen to let the child go. In truth, I daresay things are not very much different these thirty years later. Anyway, on that day, the Earl of Pennington became your father. He took you from that place without a moment's notion of ever taking you back. Without a single misgiving in the world, he knew that he had not made a mistake."

"And so the grave of the real Emerson Rutherford is in Moncalieri?" Emerson said, the strangeness of the idea seeming to swamp him.

"Not exactly, my boy. The name on that gravestone in that far off country is not Emerson Rutherford. As grief-stricken as your father was, he was still in control of his senses."

"And so the name on that gravestone is…"

"It is whatever name you were truly born with. I'm rather afraid that I never did know what that was. Your father did not tell me, and I did not ask."

"And so he hoped to return to England with me as his heir and his tracks more or less covered."

"No. It was actually very different." Dr. Philpott straightened in his chair and leaned forward a little, and Mary rather guessed that whatever he had to say to Emerson, he was most intent that the young man should listen to him most closely. "Your father cared very little for heirs and titles and family names. Whether or not the Rutherford line continued as Earls of Pennington was not a question which ever concerned him. In that awful summer, your father had lost the only two people in the world he had left to love. His reason for taking you home with him was *not* to ensure that the vanity of family name and family line was satisfied. Nothing could be further from the truth. Lord Pennington was a good man with much love to give, and nobody left to give it to. From the moment he took you from that orphanage in Moncalieri, in his eyes, you were his son. Not the son he had lost, but *quite another* son. And I can tell you without any reservation that that man continued to love you as a father should throughout his entire life. His only reason for concealing your identity was to ensure that you had a wonderful future ahead of you. You had been born into poverty and loss, and Lord Pennington was determined that you would never know such hardship again."

Emerson had bowed his head a little, and Mary could see that his hands were firmly gripping the arms of the chair. The skin of his hands had become taut, and each of his knuckles appeared almost white. Mary realized that Emerson was fighting emotion, not least of which was the relief that his father had truly loved him as a son. At that moment she understood just how hard things were for men, and how they always had to fight to maintain their composure. Had she not herself witnessed Emerson in the garden, only allowing a vague hint of emotion to appear simply because he had believed himself to be entirely alone? Not for a moment had he known that there was a spy watching from an upper window.

And now, in the face of something more heart-breaking than

anything he had already lived through, Emerson Rutherford was very much forced to behave like the Earl of Pennington; gripping the chair and fighting back everything his heart wished to express. Once again, Mary had to dab at her eyes, although mercifully unnoticed on that occasion.

"I'm going to call Violet to make us all some more tea," Dr. Philpott said kindly and then, quite to Mary's surprise, the elderly man rose to his feet and easily carried away the tea tray himself, in the hunt for his housekeeper. The moment he had quit the room, Mary turned to Emerson and reached out her hand.

"Emerson?" she said quietly, resting her hand on the top of his.

He did not answer with words, but with his eyes closed, he simply nodded twice, as if to tell her that he would be well any moment.

"What a lovely old thing Dr. Philpott is, and so very perceptive. He has given you a moment to gather yourself." Mary did not expect any response and was merely filling the silence and hoping to soothe him with nothing more than the sound of her voice. She was pleasantly surprised to hear a little chuckle escape from the Earl, as he finally opened his eyes and lifted his head.

"I told you he has a way with pretty young women, did I not?" He continued to chuckle. "And here now you have fallen for him too."

"I'm rather afraid I have. He is, quite simply, adorable."

"And he always was the kindest of doctors."

"And the most sensible of men, I would say. I rather think that he is telling you to let your knowledge change nothing. I think he is telling you to regard your father *always* as your father, because in truth, that is exactly what he was."

"If I am completely honest, despite the shock of it all, I never truly doubted that. I rather feared that he had come to see me as his original child, and not the child I truly was."

"Good. Then this realization alone is one good thing to come from it all."

"Yes, I believe you are right. Still, I cannot help but wonder what move I should make next. This rather stacks the cards very much in Constance's favor, doesn't it?"

"It might *seem* that way, and yet it might not *be* that way at all. You see, there is still no proof of it all or at least none that we know of."

"It is very good of you to try to keep my spirits up, Mary, but I know I shall not rest easy until I am sure that the future of my children is safe."

"I understand that. Once you are recovered from the events of this day, we shall come up with a plan, you and me, and we shall get to the bottom of it all, yet."

"Thank you, Mary." He turned his beautiful blue eyes upon her and turned his hand from gripping the chair in order that he might hold tightly to her own.

A loud cough mixed with a mischievous chuckle in the doorway signaled the return of Dr. Philpott. As his shrewd eyes fixed upon their joined hands, the old Doctor retook his seat, and smiling broadly at them both he let out a hearty chuckle.

CHAPTER 11

*I*n the days which followed, Mary very much re-
joined the household as an active member.
Despite the protestations of Mrs. Miller and Emerson
himself, Mary knew that she felt fit and healthy, and was
extremely keen to have the children back in her charge.

As much as it was clear to her that Oliver and Isobel had
missed her greatly, it was also obvious that Daisy had done
an exceptional job with them. They had developed rather a
fondness for the young maid, and had insisted upon visiting
her in her duties every day.

Mary had been highly amused at their keenness to polish
everything in sight, and Daisy had truly been very glad to see
them. Mary could see that she would undoubtedly have to
add a small amount of polishing to their already growing list
of daily activities.

On the third day in which they had found Daisy at her work
in the drawing room, Oliver and Isobel had happily set about
polishing a small side table. Already gleaming, it was clear

that the children had polished that particular piece several times before.

"They do seem to love it, Miss Porter," Daisy had said, somewhat shyly.

"They do indeed, Daisy. In fact, they have talked of little else since I returned to them. They very much enjoyed their time with you, and I am uncommonly grateful for your care of them."

"Oh, they were a pleasure, Miss," Daisy said, clearly with honesty.

"I say, children, perhaps when you have finished in here, you might like to come into my study and polish my desk for me."

Mary spun around to see that Emerson had come into the room. Daisy hurriedly dropped a small curtsy, and quietly resumed her duties. Oliver and Isobel looked up from their determined polishing with bright, happy little smiles. Mary could see from the look on Emerson's face that he had not entirely been expecting such an open and ready reception from the tiny twins.

"I think that sounds like a very nice idea, children, don't you?" Mary said, ruffling their light blonde hair.

"Yes, Miss Porter," Said Oliver, somewhat loudly.

"We could make Papa's desk really shiny," Isobel added, already gathering up Daisy's dusters and a tin of beeswax polish. Mary gave a little shrug to Daisy, silently asking if they could relieve her of those items for just a little while. Daisy smiled warmly at the children, then nodded her ascent at Mary.

"Come along then, children. There's no time like the present," Mary said, as she gently led the children out of the drawing room.

Once inside Emerson's study, Mary stared, wide-eyed, at the sheer amount of paperwork and chaos on the Earl's desk.

"Oh," Emerson said, almost as if it was as much a surprise to him as it was her. "I daresay I ought to move these things first, had I not?" He spoke as much to the children as to Mary, and she could feel her heart opening wider than ever it had done before.

"Yes, Papa. You know that we shan't be able to polish it until you do," Isobel said, her little hands firmly on her hips as she began to advise her father on how best to clear his desk. Both Mary and Emerson laughed heartily at the adorable little girl, and even Oliver joined in, although Mary was fairly sure he had no idea what he was laughing about.

"I say, Isobel. You are a marvelously bossy little thing, aren't you? I'm afraid I had quite forgotten that." Emerson reached down and scooped his little girl high into the air as she giggled and squealed delightedly. "You remind me rather of your dear governess," he said, with a mischievous laugh.

"Lord Pennington!" Mary said, in mock chastisement. Emerson eyed her closely, and Mary very quickly realized that he was indicating that she herself had her own hands on her hips. Reddening a little, she shook her head, silently surrendering.

"Me too, Papa! Me too!" Oliver had raced over to his father and was bouncing frantically at his feet. Emerson swooped down and lifted his other child with ease, smiling with the purest happiness as his tiny children wrapped their arms around his neck. Mary silently warded off any appearance of tears, joyful or otherwise. She rather thought she might have to have a word with the Earl of Pennington about his disastrous effect upon her hitherto entirely steady emotions. What would her father have said if he'd had any idea how many times Mary had been forced to blink hard in the last few days? He would certainly find it all very amusing, she had no doubt.

By the time his desk had been cleared and his children were earnestly polishing it, Emerson's countenance had resumed just a little of the tightness of recent days. Making his way over to the large window in the corner of the room, Emerson indicated with his eyes that Mary should follow. For some moments, they looked out upon the countryside, making rather general and pointless comments upon it. Hearing that the twins had struck up some small conversation of their own, Mary nodded at him, rather indicating that he should speak freely, if somewhat quietly.

"Mary, now more than ever, I have resolved to do whatever I can to keep my children safe. I really must come up with a plan of some sort, and soon. But I should very much like to do that with your help since you rather seem to be the smarter of the two of us," he added the last with the smile that seemed to be making itself known more and more, and Mary found herself rather enjoying its familiarity.

"Oh, well, that surely must be true, for I already *have* a plan formulated," she said, casting the briefest of looks at the children to ensure that they were still fully occupied.

"Indeed?" His blue eyes seemed to brighten the wider they opened, and his countenance was all astonishment. "Is there time for you to tell it to me now?"

"Yes, Emerson. I plan to make my own visit to Italy."

"Italy?" Emerson spoke the last so loudly that Oliver and Isobel stopped their polishing and looked over.

"What is Italy?" Oliver asked, addressing the question directly to his father.

"It is a country, my dear boy. It's very much like England, but warmer."

"Oh." Seemingly completely satisfied with the ridiculous answer, Oliver returned to his polishing duties, and his sister resumed her conversation.

"You mean it, don't you?" he said, in a very much lower voice.

"Yes, of course, I mean it. Between us, we must come up with some reason for my departure. It must be something that sounds extremely credible. Anyway, that is a side issue. I have been making some inquiries into travel, and have discovered that it shall be very much quicker to do the whole thing by sea. It should take anywhere between two and four weeks to make the voyage, whereas if I took a short sea crossing and completed the journey by land, it could add up to a further two weeks. Not to mention the fact that it will be grossly more uncomfortable traveling by coach in mountainous regions," Mary said it all so matter-of-factly that Emerson could do nothing but look at her, his mouth agape.

"But Mary…"

"I have thought it all through, Emerson, and it is the only way; seemingly, that your long dead butler and Dr. Philpott are the only people who have any knowledge of your origins. Since Dr. Philpott has kept your father's confidence these thirty years, I cannot begin to imagine that anyone should ever wrest the truth from him. Therefore, the only source of

proof in this country is that wonderful, adorable old man."
Mary still could not help but smile whenever she thought of
Dr. Philpott's twinkling eyes.

"And you intend to discover if there is any proof whatsoever
in Italy?"

"It is the only course of action, Emerson. There is no proof
here for us to find and deal with. If there is any proof at all,
then it clearly lies in Moncalieri, and so that is where I
intend to go. In fact, there is a sailing from Southampton in
just three days. So, we really must come up with a suitable
and believable explanation for my sudden and lengthy
departure."

"But Mary…"

"And I beg of you, please engage Daisy to look after the
children for me. Miss Morgan seems perfectly content to
wander about Linwood without a responsibility in the world,
and I should not seek to change that."

"Well, yes, of course," the Earl said, nodding. "But wait a
moment! You have me very nearly agreeing to all of this," he
said as if Mary's segue into the arrangement of care for his
children had been a rather clever device for her to skate
around any objection of his. In truth, that had been very
much her intention.

"But you must agree to it. There is no other way. And in any
case, I can fund the whole thing for myself, if you remember
rightly. In truth, there really is nothing to stop me." Mary
gave him a little smile, and rather comically rested her hands
upon her hips again.

"So I see." The Earl smiled broadly, as he surveyed her hands
on her hips rather longer than might be considered decent.

Mary found herself feeling a little flustered by the intensity of his gaze; flustered, but not displeased.

"So, it is settled then?" Mary asked, keen to have the thing agreed.

"It is settled, Mary. But with one, solitary, fly in the ointment."

"And that is?"

"I am coming with you."

"But you cannot!" Mary said, her eyes wide.

"Why not? I shall behave myself, you have no fear of me."

"That was not my concern." Mary could not help but laugh, and hurriedly put her hand over her mouth lest the children should hear her.

"Then what?"

"From what you tell me, your wife resides not far from Moncalieri, correct? What if she should see you? Surely she would deem it an attack, and race to carry out her threat in any way possible." Mary looked at him, raising her eyebrows for confirmation that he had understood what she was saying. "Whereas, I am an unknown quantity. For me to be in the area is as nothing to her. I am completely unrecognizable and could work in total secrecy. Surely you see the sense in what I'm saying?" Mary said, whispering rather desperately.

"Yes, what you say makes perfect sense." He smiled at her, nodding in a way which falsely led her to relax. "And so I shall wear a most cunning disguise. And I shall masquerade as your husband, Mr. Porter. Yes, *Mr. Porter*, I think that suits me, do you not?"

"But you cannot!"

"Not only can I, but I shall. As bossy as you are, Mary Porter, I simply shall not see you traveling to Italy all alone. You are a young and beautiful woman, and I shall not see you risk your neck simply to save mine."

"But…."

"There is no *but* about it, Mary. I shall be accompanying you, and that is that." He fixed her with a determined stare and then gave her such a long and slow smile that she felt it almost as a physical touch. "So, you see, I can be rather determined and bossy myself."

* * *

As she walked around Southampton docks, Mary could hardly believe that it had only been days since she had come up with her plan. Emerson had rather cleverly come up with a plausible reason for Mary's sudden and lengthy absence. After a very brief conversation about her family, Emerson decided that the rest of the household must be told that Mary had been called away to be with her sister. It was true that Katherine Beckleham, the Duke of Arleton's young wife, was indeed expecting their first child. With the pregnancy in its very early stages, Mary had allegedly been sent for as a companion to her sister, who was feeling rather unwell and taking the whole thing quite badly.

Mary was rather impressed with Emerson's idea and thought the scenario a not uncommon one for the times. As she had spent the preceding days packing, she had been confidentially informed by Mrs. Miller that the Earl himself was finding it necessary to make some trip or other. He had rather intimated to her that he needed to go abroad, in connection with Lady Pennington. In truth, he need not say any more, for none of his household would have expected it of him. It was simply enough that he had expressed his need to make the journey, and alluded vaguely to its purpose.

As Mrs. Miller confided in her, Mary could not help but feel a terrible guilt at the idea of somehow betraying her dear friend. However, she could not possibly break Emerson's confidence, even though she knew with all her heart that Mrs. Miller would never breathe a word of it. Despite this guilt, she found she could not say... that she could not break his confidence.

When she thought about it sensibly, Mary very much realized that Mrs. Miller was a good and kind person who would, had she been aware of the circumstances, have fully understood Mary's need for deception. At least that thought eased her mind.

As part of their planning, Emerson and Mary had agreed that he should be the first of them to leave, but only after first announcing Mary's need to go away herself. They rather gathered that, by mixing the circumstances up in such a way, that they could only be seen as pure coincidence. In truth, there was none at Linwood Hall who would have any suspicion of the closeness of their friendship.

* * *

ALL IN ALL, Mary had rather enjoyed making her own way from Linwood to Southampton. In truth, she was not unaccustomed to traveling alone, and even the idea of traveling to Italy unaccompanied had not concerned her in the slightest.

Mary was a truly bright and capable woman and had a

reasonable grasp of the Italian language. However, she had been sure to pack a small English-Italian dictionary which she had found gathering dust in the great library at Linwood Hall. She was a good planner and did whatever she could to leave nothing to chance. Discovering that the Earl understood not one word of Italian gave Mary rather a thrill. That she would be the main communicator rather gave Mary the impression of being in charge, and she had laughed at herself for being all that her father proclaimed her to be.

The docks at Southampton had been filled with noise and people, and everywhere she looked great cargoes were being shifted here and there, ready to be packed into the ship, which was so vast that it almost seemed to rob the docks of a skyline.

Her trunk having been packed and sent ahead of her, Mary was left to carry nothing more than a lightweight case and her reticule. Mary paused on the docks and took the opportunity to look about her, taking in all she could of the hustle and bustle of lives and livelihoods. The place seemed to hum with excitement and she found her stomach turning in sympathy. Mary had never sailed anywhere before, and in truth, had never left England. As she stared up at the great ship, she rather hoped that she would not suffer too terribly from seasickness, something she had heard could be quite appalling.

Finally, it was time to board. As Mary approached the great vessel, she looked up at it and wondered where exactly within its great structure Emerson might be. The plan had been that he would board the day before, and spent much of his time getting his bearings and searching through the passengers for any sign of an acquaintance who might recognize him. Mary thought, but did not say, that it was rather a fortunate thing that Emerson had always led so solitary a life. In truth, there was very little chance of Lord Pennington being recognized aboard a packet steamer bound for Italy. Still, he had been determined to leave nothing to chance, and Mary silently applauded the fact that his approach to planning was equally as thorough as her own. So much so, in fact, that he had insisted upon starting a beard even before he embarked on the journey from Linwood to Southampton. For two days straight, before leaving Linwood Hall, the Earl had ceased to shave. Mary was rather surprised to note how quickly the rough stubble began to appear on his smooth features. She was also surprised to see that the hair on his face was very much darker than the light brown and blonde of his head. All in all, although Mary was not entirely fond of beards, she found the effect upon Emerson was actually rather handsome.

Mary was amongst the people who had arrived for the sailing at very nearly the last minute and felt rather jostled as she began to board. Furthermore, the tide was very well in, and the ship sat so high out of the water that the climb to board it felt somewhat vertiginous.

She had been aboard ship not more than two minutes before she perceived an ever more thickly bearded Emerson striding towards her. The sight of him set her heart a pounding and brought the heat of a blush to her cheeks. My, he was handsome.

"There you are, my dear." He strode towards her, holding out his arm for her to take. Clearly, he was already in the character of *Mr. Porter*, her husband. He had booked them onto the ship as such, and Mary had, more than once, felt slight misgivings about their rooms. What would happen to her reputation if it was ever discovered? Shaking her head slightly she put those thoughts aside. Thinking of the task at hand, she knew she had done what was needed and therefore, did what she could to dispel her concerns.

"I must say, Mr. Porter, that beard of yours would seem to grow faster than Russian vine," Mary said, a light smirk on her face.

"Yes, it does, doesn't it? But it forms rather a good disguise, does it not?"

"In truth, Emerson, you rather look exactly like yourself, but with a beard." Mary began to laugh.

"Well, I should have expected rather more support from my wife, Mrs. Porter. Anyway, I have packed some truly dreadful outfits, and I challenge you to recognize me in any of them."

Mary laughed again. Emerson's high spirits were truly infectious. She began to wonder if he had rather lost sight of their reason for going, or if he was simply deferring the emotions in lieu of three weeks' respite at sea. Either way, Mary felt uncommonly gratified to see that some of the tension had clearly eased its way from his countenance.

OVER THE NEXT FEW DAYS, Mary found she rather settled in. She had been uncommonly relieved to discover that she did not, after all, suffer from seasickness or any hint of motion sickness at all. Emerson did not seem to suffer either, and Mary rather liked the idea of such a fortuitous start to their undertaking.

The compartment which Emerson had booked them comprised several rooms. Most importantly, there were two bedrooms, the smaller of which Emerson took without a moment's question. That simple gesture filled her with warmth. Here was an Earl giving her the better room!

Although it had felt a little strange at first to be in such close quarters, it very quickly became comfortable and familiar.

In truth, those few weeks at sea had felt like a rather wonderful little holiday in which they spent their time reading, walking the decks, and playing at various word puzzles. They had spent much time talking about their respective childhoods, although Mary's tales of family were, quite naturally, rather longer than Emerson's. Still, he seemed not to mind and gave every appearance of enjoying finding out more about her and where she had come from. He had listened with excited interest as she told him the tale of how her older sister had been proposed to by a Duke on the very day that her father had inherited the entire fortunes of the Stonewell Shipping company. Each day she felt her heart opening more and more. Just the sight of Emerson had her heart pounding and the breath catching in her throat. When she took his arm, a delightful heat would spark from the contact, and she spent all her waking hours thinking about him and his plight.

The voyage had, more or less, run to schedule, and they were nearing the coast of Italy in what had felt like no time at all. On the morning that they were due to dock, Mary and Emerson had stood on the deck watching dry land grow ever closer.

"I rather wish this voyage wasn't coming to an end, Mary," Emerson said, his eyes staring off across the sea.

"Yes, it's been rather fun, hasn't it?" Mary said, surprised to learn that Emerson might well be feeling as flat as she herself did. "And I suppose now that we can see Italy before us, there is some trepidation for you about what is to come."

"In truth, there is that, Mary. But my sadness for this part of our journey ending is not really concerned with that." Emerson turned to look at her face, his shining blue eyes seeming to pour into her own.

"Oh?" Mary wanted desperately to know his meaning, and equally desperately did *not* want to know.

"It's been like a lovely sort of a daydream, hasn't it? Well, it certainly has for me. You see, I've rather wished I *was* Mr. Porter; not *Lord Pennington*, not *the Earl*, and not the nameless orphan whose gravestone lies over that way." He indicated the approaching land with a flick of his eyes. "Just Mr. Porter, on a wonderful trip to Italy with his beautiful wife, Mrs. Porter."

"Emerson," Mary quietly objected.

"Mary, I do not wish to make our mission together somewhat uncomfortable, and yet I must tell you how I feel."

Mary could not speak. She had a very good idea what was coming and was almost afraid to hear it. Not afraid because she did not return his feelings, but afraid because she did. Her breath seemed to catch in her throat, and her heart pounded in her chest, and the world seemed to stop.

"You see, Mary, I've really rather fallen in love with you. Not just because you're helping me, not just because I have been able to confide in you and nobody else. It's everything about you; your intelligence, your bravery, your hands on your hips and that incredibly sharp little tongue." He smiled at her, and Mary could not help but laugh. For such a taciturn man, Emerson really was rather funny. "Add to that your extreme beauty and your unwavering care for my children, and you must see that I could not help but end up feeling as I do."

"Emerson, you mustn't." Mary did not know what else to say. Her heart and soul seemed to burn for him, and yet she could not speak the truth of it.

"Tell me, Mary, that you do not feel some love for me." Emerson took both of her hands in his own. Mary did not object; they were on a ship far from home, and entirely incognito as husband and wife. There was no one at that moment to pour judgment and shame upon them.

"I do love you, Emerson. I love you dreadfully. But you have a wife, and I cannot dwell upon my feelings, for I know that it can never be."

"I know. But there is always a way around things," he said, a certain amount of hope in his eyes.

"Emerson Rutherford!" Mary exclaimed, her eyes full of offense.

"I really do not know what you were thinking, my dear woman, but I was simply dwelling upon the idea of obtaining a divorce from Constance." A broad smile slowly began to appear on Emerson's face. "Tell me, Miss Porter, what exactly were *you* thinking?" The merriment in his eyes told Mary that he knew very well what she had been thinking, and she could have stamped on her own foot as she felt her cheeks flush in complete embarrassment.

"I… well… I…" Mary began, trying to ignore his good-humored chuckling. "I think you might find a divorce rather hard to come by, Emerson. In fact, I think you shall find it next to impossible."

"Yes, I know it is not in the common way of things, but the fact is that such things do exist, and they can be obtained."

"But how?"

"I rather think one has to petition the Church of England for such a thing."

"Yes, I believe that is the way. However, I think that they do everything in their power to prevent such a thing, and you might very well find that it shall take you years if it ever happens at all."

"But one must have hope, Mary. I think I have a very good case, since my current wife has been committing adultery in a foreign country for more than twelve months, has abandoned her own children, and since the church is often swayed by such vanities, the fact that I am an Earl might go a long way." He shrugged as if he had just thought of that last thing. "That is, of course, if I am still an Earl upon my return to England."

"Emerson, you must have hope and faith. We shall do everything in our power to ensure that you and the children keep Linwood Hall, and you must not forget that."

"Then you must have hope and faith that I can find some means by which to obtain a divorce, even if it does take a while."

"A while? It could take years and years, Emerson."

"I promise you, Mary, I am most decidedly worth the wait." It was some moments before he furnished her with his most mischievous grin. He had spoken so seriously, that Mary had hardly recognized the joke, and she had solemnly nodded in agreement until the meaning of it all had dawned upon her.

"You really are much sillier than anyone would suffer to believe, even if I swore it upon a Bible!" Mary chastised him, before stepping forward and lightly laying her forehead upon his chest. If they could have no more time together than those few moments on board that ship, posing as man and wife, then Mary would take what she could get. Emerson had automatically wrapped his arms around her, and she had returned his embrace without shyness or reticence.

* * *

THE ROOMS they had taken in a sumptuous guesthouse in the small and quaint town of Moncalieri were almost as large as the ones they had enjoyed aboard the ship. Despite his declaration of love for her, Mary was relieved to find Emerson every bit the gentleman he had been from the moment they had met. Once again, he had taken the smaller of the rooms to call his own and had not again approached the subject of love, divorce, and marriage, as they had discussed on the ship.

Mary was rather pleased that he had given her essential respite from such thoughts. In truth, she knew she had a great task ahead of her, and she would need all of her concentration to complete it.

Despite the truly appalling length of his month-old beard, Mary still insisted that Emerson kept to their rooms as much as possible. Whatever awful clothes he wore, and however long that beard grew, Mary surely knew that Constance would have recognized him immediately. She had been married to him, and they had produced Oliver and Isobel together. Mary knew that there was little to no chance that a woman who had known a man so well, albeit briefly, would be fooled by the simple addition of a beard and a rather poor dress sense. In truth, the disguise of which he was so proud, rather drew attention to him and, try as she might, Mary could not make him believe her upon the subject.

"But surely I can help? Perhaps I could visit the grave of poor, dear Margaret Westbury?" He had begun on the second day, obviously keen to quit their rooms for a while.

"But why, Emerson?"

"To see who is buried beside her. I should very much like to try to find my gravestone. Or, should I say, Emerson's gravestone." He looked down for a few moments, clearly pondering what he just said. "It's all so complicated, isn't it? I mean, despite having the truth of it all from Dr. Philpot, still, I consider myself to be Emerson Rutherford."

"Because, I suppose, the reality of it is that you *are* Emerson Rutherford. Not the Emerson Rutherford who died here as a child, but rather the Emerson Rutherford who was born here on the very day that his father walked away from the orphanage with him."

"Yes, as always, Mary, you rather make sense." He smiled at her and sat back down in his seat. "Well, I suppose you had better leave me a book to read, or some other form of amusement if you are going to be leaving me here alone for the entire day again." His rueful smile made Mary laugh, and she returned to her packing trunk to see what books she had which had not already been devoured by him.

"I'm afraid that all that is left is one romance novel. You have read all the rest on the sailing."

"And I shall take it and be grateful. In any case, I am by no means opposed to romance."

"I cannot help but think that, when I first met you, that was the one sentence that I never thought I would ever hear you say." Mary laughed as she tied the ribbons of her bonnet, and reached for her lightweight cloak.

"And who can blame you? I rather thought something similar myself." He smiled as he opened the little novel to its first page.

"Well, wish me luck," Mary said, making for the door.

"Good luck. I do hope you get on better than you did yesterday."

* * *

As Mary set off through the narrow streets, she absently squeezed at the body of the little velvet drawstring bag which hung on her wrist, with the intention of ensuring that she had remembered to bring her English-Italian dictionary. So far she had managed to get along with the words that she knew. However, there had come several sticking points in her inquiries, and the little dictionary had rather proved itself invaluable.

It had taken her some time to wrest any information of local orphanages from their surly landlady. Given that their accommodation was so comfortable, clean, and modern, Mary had been rather surprised to find that the landlady was seemingly so very disinterested in her guests.

Not only was she disinterested, but the dreadful woman was also rather mistrustful. Quite what she suspected when Mary had been asking her about local orphanages, Mary could not begin to imagine. In the end, it had been necessary for her to tell some truly terrible lies. When she seemed to be getting nowhere with the landlady, Mary had rather forced her eyes to well up and explained in broken Italian that she and her husband, finding themselves childless, had finally decided upon the idea of taking in an orphan and raising it as their very own child.

A last-ditch attempt had, finally, elicited some information from the woman, if not a single shred of sympathy. However, Mary quickly reminded herself that she was, indeed, lying to the woman, and as such had no right to sympathy of any kind, in truth.

The woman had told Mary that there were three orphanages in the area but had only given her directions to one of them. When Mary had asked for the further two, the woman had simply shaken her head in a somewhat exasperated fashion and strode away from her. Deciding to waste no more time contemplating the source of the woman's dreadfully peevish behavior, Mary thought that someone working at the first orphanage would very likely be able to direct her to the other two.

She had, of course, been right on that matter. When she had visited that first orphanage the day before, she had been furnished with rather thorough directions to the other two. However, as she had gently made her inquiries regarding the adoption of a blonde-haired, blue-eyed infant some thirty years before, she had been met with a great deal of confused silence.

After a lengthy and somewhat convoluted conversation, Mary had learned that none of the current staff were old enough to have worked in the orphanage thirty years beforehand. In truth, most of them had not even been born at that time.

Furthermore, her inquiries as to the keeping of records were met with a certain amount of suspicion. It took a great deal of time to assure the staff that she was not, in fact, either criticizing or investigating their running of the orphanage. She simply had an urgent and pressing personal matter which must be cleared up. Feeling the need to give them a little more information, in the hope of gaining their trust, she had explained that she was interested in any details of a wealthy English man adopting a small blonde Italian orphan boy in 1795. Without actually saying the words, Mary rather intimated that the wealthy English man had, indeed, been a relation of hers. Finding herself to be a consummate actress, she lowered her gaze a little, indicating that she was far too embarrassed to go any deeper into the story. Their curiosity notwithstanding, her tale had, indeed, served to make them believe that her inquiry was a simple private matter and that there was nothing official about it.

It was then openly explained to her that the keeping of records had only begun in 1815, some twenty years later and that even *those* were rather sketchy in part.

Mary had thanked them most effusively and had taken the rather substantial amount of money from her velvet drawstring bag and handed it to them in a donation. In truth, Mary hoped, rather than believed, that all of the money would be used for the children. Nonetheless, it had secured her very detailed directions to the remaining two orphanages.

HAVING LEARNED something from her dealings of the day before, Mary broached the subject of a monetary donation much earlier on in her conversation with the second orphanage. They had been so very pleased with the sight of the money that Mary had been ushered into a small office, furnished with the most appallingly strong coffee, and shown the rather poorly kept register of adoptions in their keeping. It was clear that the second orphanage had also not kept any form of paper record until well into the 1800s. Again, there was no person working there who had, indeed, had any knowledge of the orphanage in 1795. Once again, all present were rather too young to have been working in an orphanage at that time.

As Mary made her way to the third and final orphanage, she tried very hard to see her lack of progress as a good thing. And in truth, it was. Two out of the three orphanages had no paperwork and absolutely no knowledge of the wealthy Englishman who had adopted a small, fair Italian boy thirty years previously. *Of course, it was a good thing*. It was a *lack of proof*, and if Mary could not find any, then Constance Pennington could find none either.

ALTHOUGH SHE WAS TIRED, it was only early afternoon, and Mary rather thought that she should make her way to the final orphanage. It would be extremely gratifying to be able to return to Emerson and tell him that not one shred of proof existed on this earth of his parentage.

Her visit to the third orphanage felt like déjà vu. The very moment that she had proffered a donation, she was once again furnished with as much information as the staff could provide. Fortuitously, Mary had not been offered any more eye-watering strong coffee.

As the staff recounted very much the same sort of circumstances as the previous two orphanages, with regards to paperwork and the keeping of records, Mary could feel her spirits on the very edge of soaring.

Once again, she recounted the tale of the wealthy Englishman and the small, blonde, Italian orphan, and once again there seemed to be none there with any knowledge of the situation.

Finally, with her thanks genuinely given and her donation made, Mary quit the orphanage and began to make her way back towards her accommodation.

However, as she had made her way along two streets, she was suddenly aware of a heavily accented female voice behind her.

"Miss? Miss?"

Mary turned around, completely surprised to hear the words spoken in English. Hastening towards her was a woman with rather a concerned look upon her face. She had beautifully thick and shiny black hair, which was fastened so loosely that the majority of it seemed to fly all about her as she ran. She had the rich and dark good looks of the Italian woman and seemed to Mary to be no more than forty-two or three-years-old.

"Miss, forgive me for chasing you." The woman had reverted to Italian but had rather kindly spoken slowly enough for Mary to easily keep up with her.

"Please, do not worry, madam." Mary's spoken Italian was also slow but by necessity rather than design. "What is the matter?"

"I work at the orphanage, Miss. I heard a little of what you were saying to my employers."

"About the little boy?" Mary's heart began to thump uncomfortably.

"Yes miss, about the little, blonde haired boy. He was here," she said, almost in a whisper, as she hurriedly looked about her for the sign of any witness.

"But I thought all of the staff were too young to have worked there at the orphanage thirty years ago." Mary was truly confused. It was surely impossible that this woman would have been old enough.

"I have only worked at the orphanage for three years, Miss. But I *did* see him, and the man who took him away. You see, I did not *work* at the orphanage in seventeen ninety-five. I was an orphan there."

"Goodness me," Mary said, her eyes wide in shock.

"But you see, I could not approach you before because there are none I work with who are aware that I was an orphan in that very place. I don't know why I have never told them, and yet I still do not want them to know. And that, Miss, is why I have chased you."

"Oh, please do not worry, for I shall not let your secret out," Mary said, truthfully. "But can you tell me what you remember of that time?"

"Oh, I remember everything. I remember the Englishman, with his fine clothes and his sad eyes. He seemed so determined to take little Paolo away."

"Paolo?" Mary said, feeling a lump begin to form in her throat.

"Yes, little Paolo Sargese. I shall never forget him as long as I live. I was just twelve-years-old myself, but I remember his face as if it was yesterday. You see, he really was the most beautiful and adorable little boy, and for all the time he was at the orphanage, I carried him around as if he was my very own. My heart was broken on the day the Englishman took him away, and yet I rejoiced because I knew he would have a wonderful life with that dear man."

"Had he been at the orphanage all his life?"

"Yes. His father had died before he was born, and then his mother died giving birth to him. It was so sad; he had never known his parents. I am lucky, I have some small picture in my head of what my mother looked like before she died."

"I'm so very sorry." Mary could not help the tears which came. Everything the woman had told her seemed to be breaking her heart, including the woman's own story.

"Tell me, did Paolo go on to have a happy life with the Englishman?" Once again, the woman looked about her to ensure that they were alone.

"He did have a happy life. He still has a happy life. In fact, the Englishman left him with a beautiful home, and he loved him very dearly. But Paolo has a problem now."

"But what is the problem?" The woman looked genuinely concerned for the life of the grown man whom she could only remember as a tiny blonde infant.

"Somebody close to him is threatening to produce evidence that he was originally from the orphanage here in Moncalieri. If they are able to do that, then Paolo shall lose his home, and he and his children shall have nothing."

"But how can they find evidence? For there is none. Apart from his dead parents, Paolo had no family. There is nobody to claim him, to single him out as their own. And as you have seen from the orphanage, there are no records of it. There is no-one who remembers, and no one who was there at the time, apart from me."

"Nobody else has approached you? A woman, I mean. For you see, the person who is out to get Paolo is an Englishwoman, like me."

"No, nobody has come. And if ever they do, I shall never tell them what I have told you. I shall take Paolo's secret to my grave, Miss." She nodded so earnestly that Mary knew she spoke the truth. "And I must ask one favor of you also, Miss."

"Yes, of course, anything."

"That you also keep *my* secret. Please, never tell anybody that I was an orphan here in Moncalieri. You see, even my husband does not know. He is from Turin, and I have led him to believe that my family passed away in recent years. He knows nothing of the poverty in which I lived, nor none of what I had to do to release myself from it." The woman cast her eyes down, and Mary did not want to contemplate what she had been forced to do to release herself from poverty.

"I too shall take your secret with me to the grave. And I swear that to God. I cannot thank you for how you have helped me today, and more importantly, I cannot thank you enough for saving Paolo again."

"Thank you, Miss. I must leave you now."

"God be with you."

"And with you, Miss. And if you ever see Paolo, please, will you tell him that Lena still loves him. That is not my name now, but that is how he would remember me if indeed he remembers me at all." And with that, the woman turned on her heels and sped away back towards the orphanage.

CHAPTER 12

*T*he sun was beginning to set as Mary and Emerson stood, hand in hand, in the large old cemetery on the outskirts of Moncalieri. It had felt to Mary to have been an incredibly long day, which had started with uncertainty, and ended with bittersweet knowledge.

Mary had hardly been able to stop herself breaking into a run, so keen was she to return to their accommodation and tell Emerson everything she had learned. The poor man had sat on the edge of his seat, desperately trying to cling onto the excited recitation of her day, complete with a rather confused chronology. Mary could almost imagine telling one of her own pupils at the Dame school to calm down and think about what they wanted to say before they spoke. Finally, she understood the excitement of a child keen to tell a wondrous tale.

It had taken some time for Emerson to actually realize that the story was almost at an end. There was no proof of his origins, save for the words of two people who had absolutely sworn themselves to secrecy.

"So, it is over," Mary had said, almost inaudibly.

"Not quite," Emerson said, as he had put on his dress coat and beckoned her to leave with him.

They had walked to the cemetery in near silence. It had been some distance, taking them almost an hour to arrive. And therefore, as they stood looking at the gravestone of Paolo Sargese, Mary had felt herself to be truly exhausted.

"So there is my gravestone, Mary," Emerson had said, rather sadly.

"No, Emerson, you are very much alive."

"But I am not Emerson, am I? I am Paolo Sargese."

"No. You *were* Paolo Sargese until a good man rescued you from an orphanage in Moncalieri. Had he not done so, there is a very good chance that two little boys would have been buried in this cemetery."

"Thank you, Mary, for all that you have done. You have helped me find out who I am, and I shall always be grateful. For all that I shall spend the rest of my life as Emerson Rutherford, the Earl of Pennington, I shall never forget little Paolo Sargese, the Italian orphan."

"Never forget," Mary said, somewhat absently. "Emerson, I have just remembered. The lady who told me that she had been with you in the orphanage, well, she asked me to tell you that Lena still loves you."

No sooner had Mary spoken the words, than she could see the sudden and profound recognition on Emerson's face. Suddenly, he raised both hands to his temples, and gently held onto his own head. His eyes were shining with tears, but he did not let them fall. At that moment, Mary knew that

Emerson Rutherford had finally gained the recollection of the time he had been Paolo Sargese. Undoubtedly it was tiny; nothing more than a suggestion of another life. He said no more than one word.

"Lena."

Slowly, Emerson dropped to a crouch and reached out with both hands before placing them flat on the gravestone of the real Emerson Rutherford.

"Thank you for the life you gave me. I promise you I shall live it well."

Mary took a few steps back, giving the man she loved the time and space to come to terms with who he really was.

* * *

ON THE DAY before they had been due to make their way back to the small Italian port to board the ship home, Mary had been reading the romance novel which Emerson had rejected as *utter rubbish* just pages into it. In truth, it was not particularly absorbing, and yet it was the last of their books in English. She rather hoped that they would somehow be able to source some other reading matter before embarking on the three-week voyage home.

"What do you think?" Emerson said, striding into the room, beardless and wearing very much more suitable clothes.

"Oh, thank heavens!" Mary put the book aside and threw her head back in laughter.

"Really? Was the beard so very terrible?" Emerson asked, his arms spread wide as if appealing to her better nature.

"Yes, Mr. Porter, it really was."

"You know, I really shall miss being Mr. Porter."

"I know you will, Emerson," Mary said, with a sad little smile.

"Mary, will you wait for me?" He did not need to say more than that. Mary entirely understood his meaning.

"Forever, if that is what it takes."

* * *

ON THAT LAST day in Italy, Mary had decided that there really was just one thing left to do. Despite some minor protestations from Emerson, Mary had settled upon the idea of traveling into Turin and visiting Lady Constance Pennington in person.

"But why? I have no wish to see her. I shall simply pen her a letter when we return home telling her everything we have discovered and letting her know she has no proof. Beyond that, I really do not think we need any further encounters with her."

"I have been thinking, Emerson. If Lady Pennington was so determined to carry out so cruel a plan against you, what else might she do? I cannot explain it fully, but I rather think I'd like to gauge for myself her reaction to the news that she has been thwarted in her attempt. I just want to see if it is likely to spur her on to greater spite, or if her countenance suggests resignation."

"I see what you mean. In that case, perhaps I ought to be the one to speak to her. I know her, after all, and perhaps I can gauge her reaction a little better."

"Or perhaps you shall lose your temper when you think of

how she left your children motherless, and say something that you will not only regret but that she shall use to fire her own determination to hurt you. Don't you see? You could so easily make things worse, Emerson."

In the end, Emerson had agreed to her visit. He had, however, insisted upon traveling the few miles with her into Turin.

* * *

BY THE TIME Mary had reached the address which Lady Pennington had sent her husband in her correspondence, she was feeling rather less confident of herself than she had done previously. On their journey into Turin, Mary could not help but imagine the beautiful, sharp, and cold woman she was undoubtedly about to face. Would she really be any match for the sort of woman who could walk away from her children without a backward glance? In truth, Mary rather doubted it.

Having persuaded Emerson to keep to a small tea room in the center of Turin, Mary had walked the last few streets on her own. The nearer she came to the address given, the more she began to feel she had made a mistake. Surely Count Costanzo could not live in such a place? As Mary looked about her, she could see that all of the houses in the area were small, dark, and rather rundown.

When Mary finally reached the front door of the house in question, she could not believe what she was looking at. It was a tiny terrace, and the wooden door was rotting, its peeling paint curling away as it dried out. The windows were small and filthy, and Mary very much doubted that a great deal of light would be getting through them. Surely something was very, very wrong.

However, Mary had come so far, and she resolutely refused to allow herself to turn back. Taking her courage in both hands, Mary knocked loudly at the door. She seemed to stand there for an interminably long time before she finally heard the tell-tale sounds of a person approaching on the other side of the door.

"Who is it?" A disembodied voice called out from behind the locked door. It was a female voice, and the words had been spoken in the cut-glass tones of an aristocratic Englishwoman.

"My name is Mary Porter, and I have come from England to speak to Lady Constance Pennington."

For a few moments, there was silence, and Mary rather wondered if the woman would, after all, admit her. Just as she had been ready to speak her name again, Mary heard the sound of laughter coming from the other side of the door. Something about its tone gave Mary rather an eerie feeling. Once the laughter had finished, Mary could hear the sound of the key in the lock. Her heart was thumping wildly as the rotten wooden door slowly opened inwards.

Mary peered into the gloom, trying to make out the features of the woman standing before her. As much as the tone of voice had clearly indicated an upper-class Englishwoman, the poor creature who stood framed in the open doorway looked anything but.

"I have come to speak to Lady Constance Pennington," Mary repeated, unable to judge the situation, nor think of anything else to say.

"My dear, Mary Porter," the woman said, wheezing a little as she spoke. "I am Lady Constance Pennington, if you can believe that."

"Oh!" Mary had heard the surprise in her voice and knew that her face must be displaying something similar.

"Am I to understand that I am *not* what you were expecting, Mary Porter?"

"I'm sorry, I…" Mary broke off, feeling truly embarrassed. At some point in the last year, the circumstances of Lady Constance Pennington had clearly changed dramatically. Not only did she appear to be living in abject poverty, but the poor woman looked to be most dreadfully unwell.

"You had better come in, Mary, and tell me why it is you have come here all this way to speak to Lady Constance Pennington."

Mary hesitated a little before stepping in through the doorway and rather regretted the fact that Lady Constance Pennington was very sensible of the fact.

As Mary followed Lady Constance through a tiny and dark drawing room out into a small and unkempt kitchen area, she could see that the woman was having the most terrible difficulty in walking.

"I'm afraid that I'm not in a position to offer you anything by way of refreshment," she said. "I can, however, offer you a seat at my kitchen table in which to sit whilst you tell me why you were bothering me."

"I am come from the Earl of Pennington, as I am sure you have already perceived," Mary said, not unkindly, as she took a seat at the grimy old kitchen table.

"And you have a message from him, do you?" Lady Pennington said, with the most dreadful wheeze. Despite her appalling conditions, and her obvious malady, Mary could clearly see the haughty defiance still burning brightly in the woman's eyes. Although she was clearly frail, there was something in that look which almost cowed Mary.

"Not entirely. Rather I have some information for you."

"Information regarding the dear Earl's parentage, I presume?" There was a certain amount of resignation in Lady Pennington's voice, and Mary rather gathered that the woman was intelligent enough to realize that there was, indeed, no proof of her accusation.

"Yes, Lady Pennington. It has been ascertained that there is no paperwork, nor any person who can attest to *any* child being removed from *any* Moncalieri orphanage by *any* English man. The proof with which you threatened your husband, Lady Pennington, quite simply does not exist."

"I'm afraid I rather thought as much," Lady Pennington said on the back of a long drawn out sigh. She spoke with a certain amount of sadness and seemed somehow to expect sympathy from Mary for not being able to find the ammunition with which to wound her husband further.

Mary felt a little anger welling within her and had been about to castigate the wretched creature when Lady Pennington was suddenly seized by an awful fit of coughing. The sound was truly appalling, almost as if her very chest was ripping open. Lady Pennington hugged herself tightly, squeezing her rib cage in an effort to subdue the obvious pain. Her pale face turned violent purple, and she was seized by the fit for some minutes. The brutal coughing drove away Mary's anger and as it continued she felt her own chest tighten. Cough after racking cough filled the little kitchen and she could see a touch of blood on the lady's hand. In the end, Mary rose to her feet, rather thinking that she must do something to help the woman. However, Lady Pennington took one of her arms from her ribs, and held out a hand, as if to stay Mary. In the last moments of Lady Pennington's coughing, Mary rather stood somewhat uselessly in the middle of the kitchen, not knowing how to proceed.

"I am all right, Mary." Lady Pennington was gasping to refill her lungs with the air which she had so painfully expelled. "Or, at least, I should say, I am all right *for now*."

"Lady Pennington, what is your illness?" Mary kept her tone completely neutral. She was keen to show neither pity nor curiosity in the matter, for fear that the awful woman would not answer.

"I have some sort of malignancy within my chest. Most likely, it is within my lungs. I do not know exactly, but the one thing I know for sure is that it is killing me."

"I am most terribly sorry, Lady Pennington," Mary said, truthfully. Although it had been clear from the woman's appearance that she was, indeed, dying, to hear it spoken aloud had somehow rather shocked Mary.

"Oh, do save your pity for someone who has the interest in it. I, dear lady, do not."

Mary could hardly believe that someone as cold and as hard as Constance Pennington had ever been married to Emerson. And yet, perhaps she had been very different then? After all, she had run from England in the expectation of a new and exciting life and had instead been met with the most dreadful misfortune. Perhaps bitterness had made her all the colder.

"All right, Lady Pennington, I shall. Tell me, should I save my pity for Oliver and Isobel?" At the moment she had said it, Mary truly regretted her spite. As awful as Lady Pennington's actions had been, Mary knew she had no right to deliver her punishment. After all, was the woman not already dying? Was she not already living alone in heartless poverty? Mary had been about to apologize when she caught sight of Lady Pennington's truly ambivalent expression.

"Was that comment designed to crush me, my dear?" Lady Pennington said, so coolly that Mary no longer held onto guilt.

"I'm afraid it was, Lady Pennington, and I'm sorry that I said it."

"It is of little matter to me whether or not you are sorry."

"But it is of great matter to me."

"Because you have higher standards, Mary Porter, I daresay."

"I have standards of my own, Lady Pennington. How they measure up to yours is of no importance to me."

"As you wish." Lady Pennington seemed almost bored.

"Are you living here alone?" Mary continued almost as if they had had no argument.

"Oh, yes, quite alone. I'm rather afraid that darling Costanzo does not cope very well with dying and decaying women. He much prefers the female of the species to be young, beautiful, and in the very best of health." Finally, Mary detected some slight emotion on the woman's face. How sad that it was the idea of the vain Italian Count which had put the emotion there, rather than the idea of her two motherless children.

"And so he has left you here alone with nothing?"

"Indeed he has, Miss Porter. Tell me, wouldn't you say I deserve it?" Lady Pennington leaned slowly across the table and peered most gruesomely into Mary's face. It took every fiber of Mary's will not to recoil from the wasted, black eyed countenance which must once have been truly beautiful.

"No, Lady Pennington, you do not deserve it. Whatever has passed before, Count Costanzo has acted most appallingly."

"Aren't you the very soul of magnanimity, Miss Porter?" As Lady Pennington slowly drew away from her, Mary could not have been more relieved.

"No, I'm not. I am simply telling you what is in my heart. Whether or not you choose to mock me for it is entirely your affair, Lady Pennington."

"Tell me, dear, what are *you* to the Earl?"

"I am your children's governess."

"Indeed?" Lady Pennington's eyes seem to momentarily brighten with wicked mirth. "And how on earth is it that a simple governess can be persuaded to make the journey to Italy to solve her employer's little problems?" Mary knew exactly what Lady Pennington was alluding to, and tried very hard not to be insulted by the insinuation.

"Lord Pennington is a very good friend of mine," Mary said, quite simply.

"Evidently." The vicious little smile was made all the more garish by the degree to which Lady Pennington's face was truly wasted.

"Lady Pennington, I do not care what you think, any more than I care to take your insinuations to heart. Whatever my circumstances, you, My Lady, are in no position to pass judgment on anybody."

"No, indeed I am not. And yet, I find it amuses me."

"Then amuse yourself, if you intend. I daresay you have little enough to amuse you now, and I am truly sorry for it." Mary's emotions were in complete flux; she was torn between despising the amoral creature before her and pitying her deeply for her terrible circumstances.

"I'm rather afraid I'm growing a little bored of you, Miss Porter," Lady Pennington began, leaning her wasted frame against the edge of the table. "And I am about to ask you to leave. Assuming of course, that you have said all you needed to say. That there is no proof that the Earl is not, indeed, the Earl, and I shall have no money after all."

"It is true that there is no proof, Lady Pennington, and no way for you to hurt your husband any more than you have done already. But it is not true that you shall have no money, for you shall."

"You seem rather more sure of that than I do, Miss Porter," Lady Pennington said, waving her hand rather dismissively in Mary's direction.

"Then I daresay you shall have to wait until you have the proof of it before you. That is a matter for yourself." Mary rose to her feet, and turned to leave the kitchen. "Please, do not get to your feet again, Lady Pennington, for I can show myself out."

"You love him, don't you?" The voice which followed her from the room had lost almost all of its mocking tone.

"Yes, Lady Pennington, I do love him."

"Then that is more than I ever did." Finally, Mary heard the resignation she had been hoping for from the moment she had decided to visit Lady Pennington. However, once it had occurred, it did not fill her with the hope and satisfaction that she had imagined it would; rather it had been one of the saddest noises she had ever heard.

EPILOGUE

*L*ady Constance Pennington had lived but six months beyond her conversation with Mary Porter. The fact that it made Mary feel rather sad was a source of genuine curiosity to her. After all, the woman had seemed unable to feel a genuine emotion for anyone on the earth, her own children included. And yet somehow, Mary had still felt a genuine sadness for the woman. Not simply because she had met with such tragic circumstances, but rather because she had lived a wasted life. A life in which she had never understood how one person could feel and care for another. The more Mary thought of it, the more she believed that Lady Pennington had not left England with Count Costanzo because she loved him. It seemed more likely to her that Constance Pennington had simply been looking for a change of circumstances, and maybe even hoping that the scandal and drama of it all would finally make her feel something.

However, in that one and only conversation Mary had ever had with the woman, she knew that it had failed; despite it all, Constance Pennington had died feeling nothing. Even the idea that she would never set eyes upon her own children again seemed not to have troubled her.

All in all, her feelings regarding Constance Pennington were dreadfully mixed. That she had persuaded Emerson to provide for the woman in her dying months had been Mary's only source of comfort in the whole thing. In truth, when she had recited the entire circumstances to Emerson, he had taken no persuading at all. Mary had been relieved at his enthusiasm in providing his wife with enough funds to make her comfortable for the rest of her life. In truth, had he not been so giving, Mary rather felt her entire feeling towards him would have changed. However, she should never have doubted him for a moment. Once she told him of his wife's true situation, Emerson had made very sure that Constance had been placed in better accommodations, and had been provided with a paid companion to nurse her until the end. The arranging of everything had meant that they had had to stay in Italy for a further week. That week was bittersweet to Mary. It was one more week of life with Mr. Porter, and she treasured every moment. And yet here he was preparing for the death of his wife... and for his journey home. The thought that things would go back to normal was hard to face. How would she ever be able to continue without her nightly talks? Without the easy and free conversation that they had developed and without his love?

Somehow, their journey home across the seas had been rather less carefree and jolly than it had been on their way to Italy.

Although, the problem they had initially set off with had been solved entirely to their satisfaction. Still, so much more had occurred in their hearts and minds on that trip that both found themselves to be somewhat more contemplative on their way back to England.

When they had arrived back in England, Mary really did go and spend some time with her sister in Arleton. As much as it had given her own and Emerson's respective stories a certain validity, she found she had rather enjoyed the reunion, not to mention a little time away to sit and think. Emerson had never spoken of divorce again, and neither of them had mentioned the fact that there was clearly going to be no need for it. They simply maintained a respectful mutual silence upon the matter, right up until, and far beyond, Lady Pennington's ultimate death.

For six months after her death, Emerson wore a black armband and kept his clothes somber.

IT WAS a year after Lady Pennington's death when Emerson found Mary in the garden. She was alone for once, taking a walk while the children had breakfast with Daisy. It was something they did at least once a week, they were still very fond of the maid.

The sun was just beginning to rise and burn off an early morning mist. The grass was wet beneath her feet, and there was a slight chill in the air. She pulled her shawl more tightly around her shoulders and then felt as if the air warmed. She had felt him behind her, it was a gentle heat, and she turned to see his smiling face. "Your Lordship, good morning."

"Good morning, Mary, will you walk with me?"

"Of course."

Emerson held out his arm and Mary looked back towards

the house, uncertain. They were hidden by the shrubbery but still she did not feel comfortable in such an intimate gesture.

Emerson chuckled beside her. The sound was like liquid sunshine, and it warmed her to her core. "Are you mocking me, Your Lordship?"

"Perhaps a little." Reaching down he took her hand in his and tingles ran up her arm.

"Walk with me." This time it was not a request but a firm but gentle command.

Mary caught her breath and walked with the Earl. All the time her heart was beating so hard against her chest she feared he must hear it.

Emerson led her to the small garden that she tended with the children. It looked a little sad in the cool morning but still the jumble of colors made her smile.

Once there he turned her towards him and took both of her hands in his. Mary felt her breath catch in her throat. She had waited so long for this moment that she dared not breath.

Emerson dropped to one knee, and Mary let out a gasp. If he did not have hold of her hands, they would have flown to her mouth. Instead, she flexed her fingers in his strong hands.

"You are not escaping," he said with a chuckle. "I have waited so long for this day. Now, as the sun chases away the mist, as it dawns on a wonderful new day, I ask that you be my wife. That your love will chase away the last of the ice from my heart. That our love together will dawn a brand-new life. My dearest love, Mary Porter, will you consent to be my wife?"

Mary let out a squeal of delight and then dropped to her

knees in front of him. "Yes," she said. "I love you so much. Yes, more than anything, yes."

Emerson pulled her into his arms and then his lips found hers. They were soft and gentle and yet filled with a yearning that she could not deny. That kiss was tender and loving and spoke of the life to come. It made her head spin and her skin tingle. It was as if he poured all his love into it.

* * *

EIGHTEEN MONTHS after the news of Lady Pennington's death had reached them, Mary and Emerson had finally married. In the end, it seemed to come as no surprise to anyone in the household, especially Mrs. Miller.

"I knew he was going to ask you to marry him, Miss Porter. You really do seem to have grown so close lately, that I could not help but see it." Mrs. Miller had smiled at her, her kindly features full of excitement as Mary had told her of the proposal. As they had sat drinking tea in the early morning, as was their custom, Mary could not help feel the familiar stab of guilt at all she had been forced to conceal from her dear friend. And yet she knew she could never, ever tell it. To let the confidence slide now would render all that had passed before truly irrelevant. And Mary knew it to be anything but that. In her heart, Mary knew that she would have to find some way to live with her deception, for it was not something that she could ever change.

* * *

THEIR WEDDING DAY, when it finally came, had been truly beautiful. Mary could never have imagined wearing so fine a gown in all her life, nor could she have dreamed of having so much attention poured upon her. In truth, Mary would not have been happy to live her life that way, but for that one solitary day, it had felt like perfection. All of her family had been in attendance, including her sister Katherine, and her husband, the Duke of Arleton. Throughout the service, Katherine had bounced her growing, chubby infant on her knee, in a bid to keep Elizabeth Jemima Beckleham quiet whilst the happy couple spoke their vows.

Oliver and Isobel, more than six-years-old by the time their father had remarried, could not have been more excited by the whole thing. They loved their governess dearly, and had seemed nothing but thrilled at the prospect of her taking over as their mother. With all of the excitement of the wedding and the attention which the twins had poured upon Mary's tiny baby niece, they had inevitably, and somewhat innocently, brought up the subject of babies. Before the wedding day was quite over, they had asked Mary at least half a dozen times if she and Papa would be having any babies. Isobel had particularly intimated that she was very keen on the idea, and would very much like a new baby to play with.

"Emerson. Oliver and Isobel are rather demanding that I produce a baby immediately," Mary had whispered into her new husband's ear as the celebrations continued all around them.

"Well, it would seem a shame to disappoint them, would it not?" Emerson said, with a bright smile.

"Yes, I rather think it would," Mary said, looking deep into his beautiful blue eyes. "That is, if you should like more children, Emerson?" They had never discussed it before, and Mary rather felt she was wandering across new ground without a map.

"Oh, of course, I would, Mary." Emerson reached out and took her hands, pulling her closely to him. "I should like that more than anything else in the world. Children are one of life's greatest blessings."

"Yes, Emerson, they really are. Oliver and Isobel in particular." Mary smiled and could not help but search for her two little angels. Seeing them fully engaged with her sister and baby niece once more, Mary laughed.

"I'm afraid I rather lost sight of that for a while, but with your love and support, I soon found my feet again, didn't I?"

"Yes, you did. But do not continue to blame yourself for it all. You had been treated very ill, Emerson, as had your children. The shock had been most complete, and it is understandable that you all went through a rather frightful period of adjustment. I can see very well that it could not be helped, and all that matters now is that you have put things right, and you have very much won back your little angels."

"You know, I rather wonder if all of that would have been achievable had you not decided to ignore your considerable wealth and search for gainful employment," Emerson said, his smile a mixture of amusement and sorrow.

"I'm sure it would have."

"And I am not so sure, Mary. I rather fear that I would have carried on in much the same way, listening to the bitter lies of a dreary old nurse, and growing ever distant from my beautiful children until it had been too late to ever do anything about it."

"Emerson, I do not believe that for a single moment. You are a good man, and you were hurting very badly, but you did not need me to show you the way back to your children. You found that on your own, whether or not you believe that to be true."

"I do love you, Mrs. Rutherford."

"And I do love you, Mr. Rutherford," Mary said, smiling brightly.

"I must say, I rather wish the musicians would stop playing and all the guests would wander away."

"Goodness me, Emerson! That sounds rather ungrateful."

"I do not mean to be ungrateful, my dear, I am simply eager to get started on the rest of our family, and all these people are rather hampering my attempts."

"Emerson!" Mary said, her cheeks flushing with embarrassment. "We do have more than just this one night to concentrate on adding to our family."

"I know we do, my love, but it is *this* night which I have been waiting for, for more than two years, so please forgive my eagerness." Emerson gave her a truly delicious smile.

"My darling husband, I could forgive you anything."

TO BE CONTINUED, find out when join my newsletter here.

PREVIEW - THE MONTCRIEFF COLLECTION

Preview - The Montcrieff Collection

Castleton, England.

1816

"Hand me those papers, would you, Grace?"

"Here, Papa." Grace leaned over the large walnut desk and laid the packet of ribbon-tied papers close to Jacob Somerville.

Jacob untied the packet and slid his pince-nez back onto his nose. Squinting, he began to sort through the papers with a puzzled look on his face.

"What are you looking for, Papa?"

"Oh, the papers of Dorothea Berenger's dowry. I know I left them here somewhere."

Grace's stomach lurched. Every time she heard that name, she felt the crack in her heart grow even wider. For so long,

Grace had refused to believe that Adam Montcrieff would really go through with the long-arranged nuptials. Grace had held firm to the belief that Adam would not marry someone he could not love, even if it *had* been the wish of his late father. Grace had never really understood how the upper classes could contrive such loveless unions for the sake of money, names and power. It seemed such a waste.

"Grace? You're staring into space child! That's hardly helpful!"

"Sorry, Papa." Grace cast sad eyes down and made a show of helping Jacob in his search for the missing documents.

"Ah, success! Here, I have them. They were on my desk right in front of me the whole time!"

Grace simply nodded at him. Every time she thought of the upcoming marriage of Adam Montcrieff and Dorothea Berenger, she could barely function. Grace had known Adam for much of her life. Jacob Somerville had been Nathaniel Montcrieffs solicitor since she was a child. Of all of Nathaniel's six sons, Grace had been closest in age and temperament to Adam. Despite her being the child of his father's employee, Adam had always treated her as an equal.

"Grace?" Jacob looked at his daughter with a mixture of frustration and sadness.

"Yes, Papa?"

"Adam is going to marry, whatever you may think of it."

"I think nothing of it, I can assure you." Grace felt her face flush.

"Grace, I am your father, so please do not think I am fooled. Since your mother died, I have made it my business to fill that awful gap. You can always speak to me of how you feel child. But please, *please*, do not torture yourself further with thoughts of Adam Montcrieff. You must know that he is beyond you."

"Papa, I *know* I can speak to you, but really, there is nothing to tell." Grace almost choked on her words as a tell-tale tear escaped from her eye and tracked its way down her cheek. Adam was not beyond her but above her in status and wealth. She was foolish to have even entertained the idea of them being together, but her heart had a mind of its own.

"Oh, Grace. Come here."

Jacob took his daughter into his arms. Grace was so beautiful and vulnerable even though she tried so hard to hide it. Pulling her close, he held her tight and then pushed her away to look at her. "You are too beautiful to be sad." Even though she was his daughter, he believed it. Any man would fall for her charms with her tall and perfect figure shown off so well in her morning dress. The high waistband floated down to a fuller skirt that seemed to be more the fashion. There were several petticoats but they did not hide her beauty, and to top it all, she had a perfect face with rich brown curls and skin like porcelain. Most striking about her were her warm eyes. Chocolate brown with hints of gold, they were honest and caring and full of warmth. How he wished that she would find the love he knew she longed for. But he feared it was too late.

So many times over the past twelve months, Jacob had silently berated himself for not noticing the bond which had formed between the two youngsters over the years. With no mother to watch her, Jacob had always taken his little daughter with him when he worked in the small office on the Montcrieff family estate. Adam and Grace had run about the grounds of that huge estate like a pair of urchins, climbing trees and paddling in the streams. They had grown up the greatest of friends, and Jacob had thought their feelings to be that of brother and sister. How wrong he had been. Only in the time since the announcement of the wedding had Jacob come to realize how his daughter loved Adam Montcrieff. What Adam himself felt, Jacob dared not even contemplate.

"Child, child. You have to let him go. Adam Montcrieff was never for you, even if he was not destined for Dorothea Berenger. It would be forbidden for him to marry a commoner."

"I know Papa."

"The Montcrieffs are aristocracy, and we are not. I am a solicitor. We live well, Grace, but we are not in their world and we never will be. You will find a good match one day, just as soon as you can shake Adam Montcrieff from that beautiful, clever head of yours."

"Oh, Papa. I know what you say is true. I know what you say is sense. But my head understands sense where my heart does not. I know I cannot marry Adam, but the sense of it all doesn't make the pain any less. I will get through it, I know I will, but you must forgive me my anguish, for I cannot help it."

"I know, child, I know."

"And Dorothea Berenger is *such* a woman! I cannot bear the thought of Adam marrying her. If he is to marry, why can it not be to someone he, at least, has a chance of happiness with?"

"Grace, you must keep these things to yourself. Dorothea Berenger is of his class, and that is *just* what they do."

"But she is so cold and calculating. She cares little or nothing for Adam, I know it."

"And I daresay the feeling is mutual, Grace."

"It seems like such a waste of a life."

"It's what his father wanted. Dorothea will bring considerable family money into the Montcrieff estate. The Montcrieffs are rich, certainly, but they stay rich with careful alliances and marriages. That is just how it works. Adam will get her money, and Dorothea will get the title her family craves."

Grace made a face, the whole idea was so completely distasteful to her.

"Grace, they play the game of life using a very different set of rules than we do."

"But how could his own father have wanted anything less than true happiness for his own son?"

"Because that is how he lived himself. Nathaniel's own marriage was the very same. Eliza brought much-needed money into the estate."

"And there was no love there either. The woman could not even force herself to weep at her husband's funeral."

"Grace, you just have to accept the way they are. In a lot of ways, despite their wealth, they will never have the same freedoms as we do. There are just some choices which will never be theirs to make, and marriage is one of them. Maybe you should find some pity in your heart for Eliza Montcrieff, instead of scorn?"

Grace thought long and hard about that. She could not imagine a set of circumstances where she would ever pity that harsh, hard-hearted old dowager. Eliza Montcrieff was a sharp-tongued snob. She and Dorothea would do very nicely for one another. Eliza was one of the aristocracies who could not see a life beyond making sure that the family name and estate survived for future generations, and Dorothea's money would help assure that. Dorothea was a privileged little madam who wanted a title, and *Countess of Castleton* was no doubt just the ticket. It seemed very pointless to Grace. It was just a prefix, and nothing more. *Miss, Mrs., Lady.* Why would somebody let their whole life be devoted to something so inconsequential? Grace never thought of Adam Montcrieff as the Earl of Castleton. To her, he would always just be Adam, her best friend. Her right arm. The only man she would ever love.

No matter what her father said, Grace knew she could never marry. How could she? Adam was the only man she would ever love, and Grace could not marry for anything less than that. Yet Adam, it seemed, could. Still, as far as she knew, Adam no more wanted to marry Grace than he wanted to marry Dorothea. He had never really made his feelings towards her known, and that hurt almost as much. Despite their years of friendship and easy companionship, Adam had never actually claimed to love her. At times, Grace grasped the reality that he probably did not feel for her what she felt for him. In her weaker, more romantic moods, Grace imagined that Adam was torn in two by his unrequited love for her. He had his duty and simply could not escape it, but Adam would love Grace as he would never love another woman. His whole life would be tinged with the sadness of a man who could never have what he truly wanted. Grace had spent many an hour in this romantic frame of mind since the wedding of Adam and Dorothea had been announced just one year before. In the weeks before Nathaniel Montcrieff had died, Adam seemed intent on doing or saying whatever it was that would see his father rest easy on his death bed. Well, he'd finally agreed to the union which had left Grace winded and on her knees in anguish.

"Grace?"

"Sorry, Papa. I will be well, I promise."

"Good girl. I have every faith in you."

"Thank you."

"I'm going to need you with me tomorrow at Wadsworth House, I've got a lot of paperwork to get through in the office and I won't manage it alone."

Grace looked stricken. Her father needed her help more and more often these days. The work was getting too much for him and she could do it just as well. For a moment, she found herself worried. What would happen when he was gone, or could no longer work? None of their clients would accept her as their solicitor, even though she was every bit as good as her father… That was a problem for another day, for now, Grace found herself torn between loyalty to her father and the protection of her own shattered heart.

"Yes, of course, Papa."

"Hopefully, Adam will be away from home. I don't want to make this any harder for you than I have to."

"I know Papa."

* * *

Tristan Ravenswood was still laughing as he watched Georgian ride away. It was a pretty sight and kept his eye

193

until she disappeared behind a copse of oak trees. Tristan then turned his stallion towards his own home, Gainton Manor.

Georgian Beckleham really was the strangest woman. Even as children, Georgian had stood out from all the others, purely because she had seemed so very odd. It was common for the children of Peers of the Realm to spend much of their childhood in association, and since the home of the Duke of Arleton had been so close to Gainton Manor, Tristan had spent much time in the company of Georgian and her older sisters.

Whilst Edith and Josephine had been much nearer his own age, Tristan had always been drawn towards Georgian. For the most part, he had gained much amusement in his efforts of teasing her. When he looked back at those days with the eyes of an adult, he could see that Georgian had always seen the world somewhat differently from the rest of the children. Whatever game it was the children played, Georgian seemed always to lack any sort of passion for it. Often, Georgian would only seem to come to life when there was some practical element to their childish games. Perhaps the building of a den, or some clever alteration or other to a toy or a game which would somehow improve its performance. In matters of mathematics and science, Georgian had always seemed to Tristan to be somewhat freakishly intelligent. It was almost as if her knowledge in certain matters was inherent, rather than taught. In truth, that was likely to be the case, since Tristan felt sure that the education of young girls did not go into much depth on such subjects.

Of course Georgian had always been so terribly fun to tease. Mainly because she never saw any practical joke coming. She just did not seem to think that way, and so Tristan had devoted much of his time to the invention of silly things to say to her, and even sillier things to do.

As they had grown into adults, Tristan had found the habit rather hard to break. With every other one of his childhood acquaintances, Tristan behaved in just the way an earl should. And yet, whenever he saw Georgian Beckleham, the child in him re-emerged, ready to come up with some plot with which to tease her. He simply could not help it.

However, these days, Tristan had to admit that Georgian had finally mastered the art of witty retort, and in that respect, he knew that she often far outstripped him. As odd as she still was, Tristan always found his spirits rising whenever he saw her, so much more so than they did with anyone else in his acquaintance.

As he sauntered along, just minutes from home, Tristan rather wondered if it was the fact that Georgian simply held more interest for him than anyone else did. There was not a mold in which you could place the girl, and if you could find one that *did* fit, it would probably not be strong enough to hold her. The fact that she had learned to fight back so admirably did not deter Tristan one iota. If anything, it increased the enjoyment of their encounters.

The one and only thing which Tristan had latterly found to be disconcerting was the fact that Lady Georgian Beckleham had grown to be rather beautiful. Despite the fact that she tended to wear rather neat and somewhat practical gowns, or even riding habits, on a daily basis. There was a certain barely-tamed wildness about her shining, chocolate brown curls and her intense, black-as-coal eyes. Her skin was a beautiful rosy cream and had not roughened, even though she was coming to spend more and more time out of doors as part of her new occupation.

Once again, Tristan found he was chuckling. The very fact that she had finally become the overseer for such a large duchy should, in truth, have come as no surprise to him. And yet somehow, picturing her determined little face as she trotted through plowed fields tickled his amusement.

* * *

"That's a lovely gown, Georgian." Edith's eyes had brightened to see her youngest sister in such a pretty shade of blue. "Is it this evening that you are going over to Theodora Bentley's home?"

"Yes, I shall be leaving shortly, Edith. I'm going in the barouche as it is such a lovely evening. That is, unless either of you will be needing it?" Georgian was fiddling with one of the lightly puffed short sleeves of her gown.

Josephine hurried over to her and arranged the errant sleeve so that it perfectly matched the other. It was not uncommon for one of Georgian's sisters to make last-minute alterations and adjustments to whatever it was she was wearing. Somehow Georgian never seemed able to show herself at her best.

"My dearest Georgian, neither of us will need the barouche." Josephine gave the sleeves a final look before nodding her approval. "Is it a literary thing tonight?"

"Yes, Theodora has a new author amongst her guests for the evening. I believe his name is Jeremy Tudor, and Theodora tells me that he has written a wonderful satire on manners." Georgian smiled happily, thoroughly looking forward to the evening's events. It was so nice to be able to have an intelligent conversation and not to be judged.

"Oh dear me, do you really think that's wise?" Edith was suddenly fluttering around Georgian like a butterfly.

"Wise?" For the most part, Georgian did not understand a great deal of what Edith said. In truth, Edith understood very little of what Georgian said either, but the two sisters had a very great affection for one another. They were so very different that it hardly seemed feasible that they would get on so well, and yet they did. Edith was a fashionable and well-turned out girl with impeccable manners. She often only ever *hinted* at a thing, and yet was usually understood by most around her. However, Georgian was very much more plain-spoken and tended to say exactly what she meant without hinting or coyness. As a result, she often had to seek clarification of Edith's meaning in conversation, and it appeared that this occasion was to be no different.

"Well, it sounds as if this book might very well be offensive. I wonder if it might perhaps be wiser to wait until you have heard what the general opinion of it is before you attend an event in which you may very well become unfortunately acquainted with the author."

"Why?" Georgian rested large and confused eyes upon her sister. Edith often thought that her sister's open confusion in certain areas was caused by a distinct lack of guile of any kind. In short, Georgian was not a judgmental person and was rarely able to understand other people's motivations for being so.

"Well, a satirical book about manners might very well be found to be poking fun at society. We do not yet know if this book is going to prove to be shocking, and so your attendance at Theodora Bentley's home might very well be noted by others in the county."

"I think I understand what you mean, Edith, but I have one observation... the people who note my attendance at Theodora Bentley's home will surely only be able to do so because *they* are also in attendance." Georgian smiled. It was Edith's turn to look confused.

"Once again, I am in the position of being required to translate." Josephine sighed loudly. "Georgian, Edith is concerned that your reputation may be harmed by attending an event which centers around a potentially controversial book." Josephine turned to Edith. "Edith, Georgian is convinced that her attendance will only be noticed by *other* attendees, and therefore there shall be nobody to gossip about her, lest they gossip about themselves."

"Oh!" Both Georgian and Edith registered their comprehension at the same time, before turning to each other and laughing gaily.

"Oh Edith, please do not worry about me. I do realize that I am quite different from other ladies, but I do not know how else to be."

"You *are* different, my darling, but I would not seek to change you. You really are the most wonderful sister imaginable." Edith stepped forward and kissed Georgian on the cheek.

"Uh-hum!" Josephine uttered loudly.

"As is Josephine, obviously," Edith said with a wicked little giggle.

"Thank you." Josephine gave a comical little curtsy to her older sister, and all three fell to laughing.

The carriage ride from Arleton Abbey to Theodora Bentley's townhouse was incredibly short. Ordinarily, Georgian liked to walk the few short miles between their houses, often cutting across the Duchy fields. However, she had dressed up for the evening, and the fineness of her gown and shoes most certainly would not permit a robust tramp through the countryside. Leaning back against the soft seats of the barouche, Georgian dreamed of the entertainment ahead. Of the wonderful words, she would hear and the bright conversation with them. How she hoped that this Jeremy Tudor *was* as controversial as Edith thought.

Georgian was very much looking forward to the literary evening at Theodora's house. Whilst she certainly *did* enjoy reading, it was true to say that she was not often drawn to the all-too-common romance novels of the day.

And so, the idea that somebody had written a satire on the subject of modern manners had rather appealed to her, and she was extremely interested to find out its contents, not to mention meeting the man who had actually written it.

There was so much about the manners which formed so integral a part of the aristocratic education that left Georgian bemused and dumbfounded. Much of what had been drummed into her over the years had made little sense and rather failed to make its mark upon her.

Georgian was truly looking forward to seeing her dear friend, Theodora Bentley. Theodora was much older than Georgian, being in her early forties. She was a rather an outspoken widow who had many gatherings of social and intellectual interest in her smart townhouse.

Georgian had first met Theodora in a tea shop in the town, as she had been sitting waiting for her two older sisters to finish their fabric shopping. Georgian had grown bored of *oohing* and *ahhing* at *this* piece of lace or *that* piece of silk, she had wandered away to have a sit-down with some tea and cakes.

When she had arrived in the little tea shop, she had sat down quietly amidst some sort of row which seemed to be going on in the corner of the room. Theodora, as she soon came to know her, was roundly lambasting Lady Cecile Lennox, the new wife of a little-known baronet of the county. As it turned out, Cecile Lennox's newfound title had gone to her head, and she had apparently been speaking to Mrs. Ledbury, the owner of the tea shop, in a most rude and abrasive manner.

At the point at which Georgian had entered the tea rooms, the little argument was well underway.

"Yes, I am perfectly well aware who you are, my dear. You are *Lady* Cecile Lennox, the new wife of Lord Gideon Lennox, and certainly not the first to be overcome by the power of her own little title." Theodora was standing in a most upright fashion, her hands resting argumentatively on her broad hips. She was wearing a duck-egg blue walking dress and a dark blue spencer which made such an imposing sight that Georgian had been unable to take her eyes from the woman.

"How dare you speak to me like that?" Lady Lennox was bristling with fury, and reddening with embarrassment.

"And how dare *you* speak to Mrs. Ledbury like that?" Theodora had not been about to back down. "And I note with interest that, *prior* to you becoming *Lady* Lennox, you always treated Mrs. Ledbury with the respect she is due. Now tell me, why the change?"

Instead of answering what Georgian considered to be a

perfectly sensible question, Lady Lennox rose hastily to her feet. She was wearing a cream overly ornate promenade dress which swished around her feet as she stormed her way out of the tea shop. Although Georgian herself had never been keen on the woman, she wondered quite what it was that she had said to Mrs. Ledbury which had so angered that dear woman's defender.

As Theodora had turned to retake her seat, she noticed the smiling face of Georgian Beckleham. The older woman smiled back, and, instead of taking her own seat, approached Georgian's table.

"I daresay you are wondering how this all started?"

"Yes, I *was* wondering what had happened," Georgian answered without any hint of embarrassment, not caring that introductions had not been made. To her, it had simply been the truthful answer.

"Oh, I like *you* already." Theodora had returned Georgian smile. "May I join you?"

"Yes, of course. I was just about to order tea and cakes, would you like some?"

"Yes, very much. Thank you." After she had made herself comfortable, Theodora held out her hand. "I'm Theodora Bentley, and it's very nice to meet you."

"I'm Georgian Beckleham, and is very nice to meet you, too." Georgian shook the proffered hand and smiled at the approach of Mrs. Ledbury. Mrs. Ledbury was beaming broadly at the woman who had stood up for her so ferociously.

"Mrs. Bentley, thank you so much for intervening on my part. I was so embarrassed, I really had no idea what to say."

Mrs. Ledbury was pink-cheeked, and her old, gray eyes were shining.

"Think nothing of it, Mrs. Ledbury. You really *do* run a most wonderful little tea shop here, and there was absolutely no call whatsoever for Cecile Lennox to make such spiteful remarks about your beautiful cakes."

"She was *rude* about Mrs. Ledbury's cakes?" Georgian's eyes were wide with astonishment. She had been enjoying the wonderfully moist and very delicious cakes since she had been a child. She could not imagine there ever being any fault to find with them. Moreover, she could not believe that somebody would say something so hurtful to such a dear old woman who had always been such an integral part of the town.

"I know, my dear girl, it rather beggars belief, does it not?" Mrs. Bentley said.

There was something about this terribly forthright woman that drew Georgian in. Georgian had always found that people who spoke their minds, and spoke them in a plain way, were so much less confusing to her than everybody else. From that moment on, Georgian and Theodora Bentley had become firm friends.

Read The Montcrieff Collection FREE on Kindle Unlimited here

MORE BY CHARLOTTE DARCY

More Books by Charlotte Darcy

Get a FREE eBook and find out about Charlotte's new releases by joining her newsletter here. Your information will never be shared. http://eepurl.com/bSNOLP

All FREE on Kindle Unlimited

Promised to the Beastly Earl

The Broken Duke – Mended by Love

The Bluestocking, the Earl, and the Author

Refusing the Duke

Now get all of The Montcrieff Novella's including an exclusive book in one 6 book collection $0.99 for a limited time and always FREE on Kindle Unlimited.

A Christmas Cavalcade of Romantic Dukes

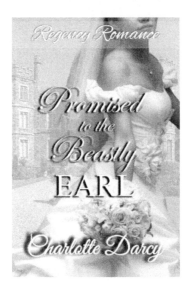

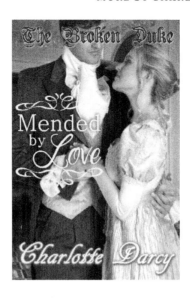

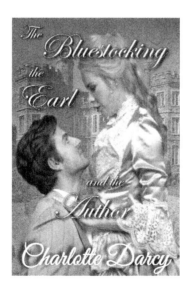

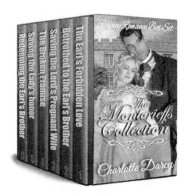

Printed in Great Britain
by Amazon